CHI CITY BOYZ
RISE TO THE TOP

ASIA HILL

Good 2 Go Publishing

CHI CITY BOYZ
Written by Asia Hill
Cover design: Davida Baldwin
Typesetter: Mychea
ISBN: 9781943686452

Copyright ©2017 Good2Go Publishing
Published 2017 by Good2Go Publishing
7311 W. Glass Lane • Laveen, AZ 85339
www.good2gopublishing.com
https://twitter.com/good2gobooks
G2G@good2gopublishing.com
www.facebook.com/good2gopublishing
www.instagram.com/good2gopublishing

ACKNOWLEDGEMENT

Wow I can't believe this is my 5th book. Time fly's, right? Well now I'm a free woman and I want to just thank all who held me down. Maria Campbell and Albert Hill. This nightmare is finally over. Thank you so much I love my parents to death. To Albert Holmes my stepfather you are an amazing man and I love you so much. Things change people change so to all those who changed on me. Thank you so much. As always this is for my 3 J's. I love you more than life itself. You know this is for you. And lastly to a very special man that came into my life Eric Jackson I'm glad that it was you. So, glad you showed me the definition of a real man. I'm ready for our journey together. I love you AVE-RICH-JO THANKS to my publishing company for riding this ride with me with no plans on stopping no time soon. I hope you guys enjoy this read. There is more to come. Thanks

ONE

Young Meech

"Every step I take, every move I make, every single day, every time I pray, I'll be missing you."
I lay in my plush California king bed in tears. I was listening to Faith Evans sing a song to her husband, Biggie Smalls. The song reminded me of my father. Today was my father's birthday, and this shit never got easier. He was everything to me. My childhood was almost perfect. I had a father that literally gave his life to provide for me, my sister, and my ungrateful bitch of a mother. My father gave that bitch the world, but what did she give him in return? She gave him death! She plotted with his best friend and set him up to be murdered. Killing him killed me. So the day I took her life made me feel whole again. I felt like I had avenged my father's death. I don't even know what made me pull the trigger. Maybe it was hurt or hate. It really didn't matter because she deserved to die. Something in me clicked after I lost Tyesha, my Auntie Shawn, and my sister, Tiki. I never thought I would be able to love again until I met BeBe. She came into my life when I was in a dark place. After Lil Man killed JoJo, I really thought about killing myself. Because of me, Tyshawn didn't have a mother no more. I was sitting in

my car at the lakefront on 79th, just a block from where JoJo was killed. I had my music playing, blunt burning, and I was downing a fifth of Hennessy. I kept replaying that day in my head every time I closed my eyes.

"Damn, JoJo, I'm so sorry," I sobbed.

I felt like I couldn't keep the women in my life safe around me. Then my mind flashed back to the night that Lil Ma killed my sister, Tiki. I wasn't there physically, but I saw it play out in my head like I was. That shit made me cry harder.

"Tiki, I miss you so much."

I started to feel like I was about to suffocate. I took another swig of the Henny to dull my pain, but to no avail. My mental torture had just begun. Flashes of my Auntie Shawn's bloody face took me over the edge. I snapped!

"LIL MAN, I FUCKING HATE YOU!"

I cocked the .38 revolver my father left me and put it to my head. I had everything I wanted: money, clothes, power, and bitches if I wanted them. Yet here I sat at the age of sixteen with a loaded gun to my head while lightly rubbing on the trigger. I wasn't happy. I felt more alone now than ever. I decided at that moment that I didn't want to live anymore.

"Fuck this shit!"

Ring! Ring!

I paused and put the gun down momentarily to see who was calling me. It was a private call. Even though I was about to kill myself, I wanted to know who the fuck was calling me privately at this time of the night.

"Who the fuck is this calling me private?"

"Um, I'm sorry, I must have the wrong number. I thought this was Manny."

"You definitely got the wrong number. Don't call this fucking phone again."

I was about to hang up, until I got a little surprise from the soft sweet voice on the other end.

"I said I was sorry for calling your phone, but you got me fucked up. I don't give a shit whose phone this is. Don't talk to me like that."

I was stuck for a second. The nerve of this bitch. First she called my phone private looking for another nigga, and then she checked me.

"You called my fucking—"

"I don't care who I called. You don't curse at me like that. What the hell is your problem?"

"So who are you, Dr. Phil?"

"No, but I am a great listener."

That was the beginning of a new beginning. Five years later, and we were still going strong. Her name is Bianca Saldavar (a.k.a. BeBe). She's a five-foot-tall, black Columbian. She's three years older than me, and I love it.

She ain't on that kiddy shit like these hoes out here be on. She's great with Tyshawn too. One day I'm going to make her my wife and the mother of my child.

I was so deep in my thoughts that I never felt her climb in the bed.

"Wipe your face, baby. I love you so much."

"I love you too, boo."

"So, Manny said that he's ready whenever you are."

Oh, did I mention that her father was now my new connect? Hell, yeah! I was getting that good ol' Colombian grade-A work straight off the boat from the port of Miami. Yeah, ya boy was doing great right now. When I first met him, he wasted no time telling me that if I hurt her, he would bury me alive. I took it all in stride though. If I was a father, I would feel the same way. He's a true Columbian kingpin with endless connections. You damn right I lucked up this time.

"So, what are we doing for your twenty-first birthday?"

"You know I'm not into all that partying bullshit! I wanna make money, not spend it."

"You worry too much. I'll take care of everything!"

Yep, ya boy was about to be the big twenty-one. I felt so much older though. At a young age, I saw too much. These days, I'd been trying to keep a low profile. I was trying to be a kingpin. That means I had to stay out of the spotlight.

"Okay, look, you can throw me a party. Just make sure it's a low-key one."

"Low-key? I'm going to throw you the best party that this city has ever seen!"

I should stick to my guns and tell her ass no party. The city is about to be turned upside down. I just hope we come out on top.

TWO

Money Man

"**M**an, you better quit playing with me before I punch yo' ass in your mouth."

"Punch who? You got the game wrong if you think you 'bout to hit—!"

Wham!

I punched her square in that smart-ass mouth of hers.

"I told yo ass quit playing with me."

"Drop me the hell off right now. I'm done with you."

"I ain't taking yo' ass nowhere. Get the fuck out."

"You just gon' put me out like this?"

"GET OUT!!"

I was tired of all this *Love and Hip Hop* drama this ho always brought my way. She grabbed her purse and got out.

"You's a stupid-ass nigga. I'm telling yo momma!"

Slam!

I pulled off and left her ass on 63rd Street. Her funky ass could take the train. *Man, my luck with bitches been terrible. I need to stay my ass off the party line.* Ever since I ran across that young ho Spooky, I was scared to commit. It'd been five years, and I was still traumatized. She was the enemy the whole time. Granted, shawty was a rider, but she just didn't have no loyalty. Man, aside from the bad luck I'd been having with these hoes, life was great! Everybody in the city knew who the hell them Chi City Boys were. There weren't no more trap houses. It was all weight now. Young's lil' wifey had got us plugged in with her pops. Shit'd been cracking ever since. I was proud of my boy. He'd been all booed up and shit. I was glad he found somebody. I just didn't trust that lil' beady-eyed bitch. If I saw any funny shit, I wasn't gon' hesitate to pop her ass.

Ring! Ring!

It was my lil' brother, Outlaw.

"What up, lil' dude?"

"Hey, where you at?"

"On the expressway, why?"

"Ride down on me. I think we 'bout to have some problems."

"What? Why?"

"Just come through."

Click!

A million things went through my mind. We hadn't had any serious issues in five years. No beef, no police, no nothing! I was always ready for whatever. I pulled up in front of Outlaw's crib and blew my horn. When my lil' brother came out, he was mugging some ugly black-ass niggas on the porch next door to his crib. Not to be outdone, I jumped out of the car to let the muthafuckas know he wasn't alone.

If they knew what I knew, they'd fix their ugly-ass faces right now before I get mad. Outlaw was just turning eighteen and still had that baby Nelson face. Looks were definitely deceiving because he was a stone-cold killer. I heard one of them say something that sounded French.

"What's good, lil' bro?"

"Shit! You see them ugly-ass black dreadlock-wearing niggas?" he pointed.

"Yeah, what about 'em?"

"Well, they from Miami, and it looks like they want some trouble."

"Trouble like how?"

"They around here selling work dirt-ass cheap, and it's garbage."

Damn, Young is about to have a fit. This is our city, and I'll be damned if I let some out-of-towners bring some shitty-ass work up here.

"We need to find out who they sold it to."

"All the lil' niggas that was around here copping from me are copping from them now. I was pulling forty racks a week easy. I'm still sitting on the last brick you gave me."

"Okay, check this out. Call everybody that copped from you and tell them that Young Meech said if they not copping from us, they not selling shit. Yo' gun rusty?"

"Hell naw! I stay ready to lick a shot!"

"Lick a shot? You been watching *Shottas* again?"

"You a hater! I'm ready."

"After I talk to Young Meech, I'ma call you back. Call School Boy Slim and tell him he might need to come up here this week. Ain't he on summer break?"

"Yeah. I'ma hit Slim up right now. Get at me later."

I dabbed him up and walked back to the car with all eyes on me. Ain't no bitch in me. I mugged their asses right back.

Ring! Ring!

I looked at my phone hoping the caller was Young Meech. It wasn't. It was my momma, Heidi.

"What's going on, Mom Dukes?"

"Don't you 'mom dukes' me! You put that girl out on the expressway?"

"Huh? What girl?"

THREE

Outlaw

We had action! I'd been quiet too long. It'd been a long five years. I had worked hard to make a name for myself in these streets. Not only would I bust my gun, but I'd also knock yo' ass out too. Boxing is like my second love. I'd been trying to keep things under control, feel me? I noticed some new faces on my block like two weeks ago. Didn't think shit of it because this is the east side of Chicago. There's so many different races. One look at them, and I knew that they were up to no good. Shit like this gets my blood boiling. I could feel it. There was about to be some bloodshed real soon. I could tell by the way they were looking at me that they thought I was some little-ass kid. That's exactly what I wanted them to think.

Let me hit up Slim before I forget.

"Outlaw, what's the word?"

"School Boy, you on summer break yet?"

"This is my last week. What's good?"

"We got some new niggas up here looking for some problems."

"Oh yeah? Where they from?"

"Miami. They rocking dreads, too."

"I wonder who they are. I'ma ask a few of my customers. What they look like?"

"Ugly. One of 'em got red dreads."

"Aw shit. There's about to be some problems."

"Who them niggas is?"

"The one with the red dreads name is Haiti Redd. He from Little Haiti out here in Miami."

"Okay, you still ain't telling me shit."

"They some dangerous ruthless-ass niggas, Outlaw. Haiti Redd got a cousin that moved to Miami from Chicago like five years ago. His name is D Money. That might be why they set up shop there. I'ma be on the first flight home."

"How you know them niggas?"

"I used to fuck with his crazy-ass sister, Khadijah. She's this crazy-ass Muslim chick. The bitch tries to hide behind Allah and her hijab, but she ain't nothing to play with. Bitch put a voodoo spell on me."

"Hurry up and get back here, man. We gon' need you."

"Tell Young and Money Man to hit up Jaw and Poohman. This shit could get real ugly."

I hung up the phone and had to go take a shit. Not because I was scared, but because 1 was ready! Two hours later I was fresh out of the shower, dressed, and ready to carry out my daily duties. I walked out of the crib feeling like the man when I walked through. I had on a black and red Bulls D. Rose jersey, of course. I don't give a fuck who don't like Derrick Rose. With or without them niggas, he gon' get a ring. Just like the Chi City Boys 'bout to put Chicago on the map, D. Rose 'bout to show up and show out in New York. I'm not a label whore like Meech and Money Man. I keep it simple with some black Levi shorts and some red and ice-green D. Rose 7s. As soon as I hit the porch, I caught that nigga called Haiti Redd staring at me. He really was an ugly-ass dude. His skin was crunchy black, and he had the nerve to have a mouth full of golds. You can't tell me shit. I know that nigga's breath smells like shit.

"Hey, lil' nigga, come here!"

Lil' nigga? Okay, I'ma let him think I'ma kid.

"My name ain't lil' nigga."

I guess he wasn't expecting my voice to be that deep or something. He had this dumb-ass look on his face.

"My bad! What's your name, shorty?"

"My name is Outlaw, and I ain't no shorty."

"Outlaw, huh? Well let me holla at you, Outlaw."

He came off his porch, followed by two money-looking-ass characters close on his heels.

"You don't need them to talk to me."

He looked at me and smiled. He snapped his fingers without looking back. They quickly turned around like robots and went and sat back on the porch. Man, who the fuck did this ol' Shabba Ranks-looking-ass nigga think he was? I wore my jerseys big for a reason. I had my .45 right where I needed it to be. If he tried anything, I was going to pop his head like a balloon.

"What's good, Joe?"

"My name ain't Joe. It's Haiti Redd."

"Okay, now that we know each other's name, what you call me for?"

"I see you look like you getting a lil' money. You slang?"

"You the police?"

That hit the nerve I was intending to hit. I saw his jawline protrude a little like he was biting down on his bottom teeth.

"I'll let that statement slide since I'm asking you about your personal affairs. You wanna make some real money?"

"Oh yeah! What you talking about?"

I could always use some extra fun bucks. Plus, I'm sure Young and Money Man would love to have an inside connect for when we shut these niggas down. Ain't nobody from out of town 'bout to move nothing on the streets of Chicago without there being some consequences. No outsiders allowed.

"I want you to run my trap house, and if you can handle it, I'll put you where you need to be."

This nigga was a straight clown. I let him think he was talking to a young-ass dummy. I was going to have fun shutting down their operation.

"All right, check this out. I'll run ya lil' trap spot, but I'm telling you now that I want in on the big shit. I got sisters and brothers to feed," I lied.

"I'll see how you do, and then we can talk."

He walked off, and I jumped in my whip. My heart was racing. This could be an opportunity or a problem. I just had to play it cool. And I was right. That nigga's breath did smell like shit!

FOUR

Jaw

Man, business was booming. It was a great idea to buy a few beauty-supply stores. Bitches buy hair more than crackheads buy dope. I was dealing with some Korean suppliers, so my shelves were always stacked. I even ran the register a few days a week. It was a foolproof cover to get my shit from overseas. Yeah, ya boy was still in the distribution business. I got that good shit straight from Columbia thanks to Young Meech's girl. The shit was so pure, you could catch a high just from touching it. We got it for the low just to turn around and bust niggas heads. I only fucked with niggas that had cake, so I didn't have no problems selling my work. I kept my business in the streets. The only thing I brought home is myself and whatever my baby, JuJu, was craving.

You heard me right. I was about to be a father again. JuJu was almost five months. These last five years ain't been a walk in the park. Even though she forgave me for messing with that crazy-ass girl Mia, she gave me hell. It felt like I had a damn parole officer. I had to do everything but piss in a cup. Finally I got tired of the detective shit. I told her if she couldn't trust me, she'd have to leave me because I was not about to live like that. I ain't had a problem since. She got her nursing degree. Now she's a part-time pediatric nurse at St. Margaret's in Hammond, Indiana. I told her she didn't have to work, but she told me she had to get on her I-N-D-E-P-E-N-D-E-N-T shit. We had also recently converted to Islam. It was time to find us a spiritual home. We attended the mosque on 73rd and Stony Island. I loved my girl so much because she was willing to learn the Islamic ways for me. She even wore her hijab whenever she went out of the house.

Ding-dong!

"Hi, can I help you?"

Speaking of Muslims, in walked this pretty-ass muslimah (Muslim woman). She was garbed up from head to toe. She had the prettiest dark-skin complexion. She was really black as hell, but her skin was smooth.

"Hi. Yes, where are your hijabs?"

"We have like over a hundred scarves over there." I pointed.

"And where is your hair dye?"

I pointed to the back of the store.

"Do you know what color you want? I could grab it for you."

"Do you have fire-engine-red?"

I was shocked. As black as she was, I knew she was not about to get no hot-ass red. She saw the look on my face and started laughing. I guess she read my mind.

"It's not for me. It's for my brother."

A nigga with fire-engine-red hair? He gotta be a queen. After she came back to the register, I properly greeted her.

"As-Salaam-Alaiku." (May the peace and blessings of Allah be upon you.)

"Wa-Alaikum-As-Salaam." (And to you be peace and blessings.)

"Hello, brother . . . ?"

"Aw, my name is L.J."

"Brother L.J., nice to meet you. My name is Khadijah."

"It's nice to meet you as well. You aren't from here, are you?"

"No, I'm originally from Haiti. My family moved to Miami when I was a little girl."

"What brings you to Chicago, if you don't mind me asking?"

"I'm up here trying to find a family member."

"Do you have any friends up here?"

"No, but I could use one."

It would be good getting JuJu's pregnant ass out of the house. Her besties were both out of town on business. Dirty took her girl to Haiti to help her mom with her charity. ReRe's crazy ass went to New York for her job. Ain't no telling when they coming back. We all been taking turns with little miss badass, Tyshawn. Even at the age of five, she was so advanced and a little too grown.

"If you would like some company, I would like for you to meet my girl, Ja'ziya. She could show you around if you don't mind."

"I would like that. I could use some girl talk."

"Good! Let me take your number. I'll have her call you tonight. Maybe you could teach her a few Muslim ways from your country."

After she left, I called JuJu and told her I found her a Muslim friend. I didn't expect her to respond the way she did though.

"Who the fuck told you I wanted or needed a new friend?"

"I just thought that—!"

"See, that's the problem. Don't think for me. Think for yo' damn self! So, you just go around looking for friends for me now?"

"Hey, you better calm all that shit down! She came in the store garbed up, and I like the way she was covered. She's from Haiti, but she now lives in Miami. Just get out of the house and get some air. You might like her. I got a good feeling about her, baby."

It was quiet, so I knew I had her.

"Okay, baby. I'll check her out. What's her name?"

"Khadijah."

"Give me her number."

After I gave her the number, I hung up feeling better. I'm always looking out for my baby. I thought my finding her a new friend would get her out of the house. I wish I never had made that introduction.

FIVE

Khadijah

"Hello? Stop calling me every freaking hour. I know what I need to do."

"Well, got it done and find her."

"If I'm not doing a fast-enough job for you, you can bring your ugly ass back up here and do it."

"You ugly."

"You are so childish, D. I'll call you when I find something. The picture I got from Facebook of Re, Dirty, and JuJu will be enough to help me. Just let me do this."

I hung up on his ass before he was able to say anything else. I knew what the hell I was doing. This was not going to be my first kidnapping. A few years after my family migrated from Haiti to Miami, I found myself in a life-or-death situation. My dumb-ass brother, Khalil, came to Miami thinking he was Tony Montana and shit. He started rubbing a few of the local niggas the wrong way. He and a few of our cousins started robbing, extorting, and killing some of the drug dealers, trying to make names for themselves. They succeeded because niggas were scared to even look their way.

They caught the attention of a kingpin named Zulu. He wasn't pleased with his workers being harassed and murdered. Being the King of Miami, he must have had a lot of clout. But let me tell you how he fucked up. He was arrogant and too damn cocky. He was always flashing his riches; he was never low-key. In my eyes he was the real target. Knowing that there was about to be a war with Zulu's crew and my family, I started watching his every move. I knew the time he took his two pit bulls for walks in the morning. I knew what day and time his wife went to the salon, the grocery store, and even to his best friend's house for her weekly fuck. I was surprised to see that shit. Apparently my brother wasn't the only nigga after his crown. So, when the two sides clashed, I was right where I needed to be. I called Zulu's phone.

"Who the fuck is this?"

"In the game of chess, it is so important to protect the king."

"What? Who is this?"

"Considering the fact that you aren't the king of Miami anymore, it's your job to protect your family at all costs. Hold on, someone wants to talk to you."

"Hi, Daddy, are you coming to get me?"

"When you decide to war with some real players, make sure that you protect and secure everything you love."

"Oh God, what do you want? You can have it all: my cars, money, jewelry. Just don't hurt my baby."

"That's exactly what I wanted to hear. You have twenty-four hours to pack the fuck up and ship the hell out of Miami. When you are ready to go, call this number. The person will give you instructions on where you can find your child."

"Well, what if I don't go?"

"Oh, you can stay if you like. I would hate to be the one to feed your little boy to the alligators in the Everglades. Oh, and by the way, your wife is fucking your best friend."

I gave him the number and hung up. Almost twenty-four hours later he came for his baby alone. I guess he left his triflin'-ass wife. Miami had a new king.

I'll do anything for my family, even if it means somebody. You don't want to fuck with us. We got family everywhere. If we want you to be touched, you will be touched. Now my cousin got me on this 007 mission in Chicago to snatch his little girl. When he first made it to Miami five years ago, with our other cousin, KeeKee, I didn't believe the story he told us. I didn't believe him until I called and found out that Auntie Julie and her boys had been murdered in a house fire. After he told us his plans, we welcomed them with open arms and taught him everything we knew. It surprised me that he was crazier than Khalil. He even put some fear in Khalil's heart. He'd never admit it, but I know he did. I saw it all in his eyes.

The older D got, the more vicious and calculated he became. Khalil and D never beefed. They just respected each other and put in work together. He gave us the whole rundown on the part of Chicago that he wanted Khalil to take over. Ironically, it's the same part of town he said his little girl would be in. We could never find pictures of her on Facebook, but he showed me pictures of the people he believed had her. This was a bad month for me to be on this kind of mission. It was the month of Ramadan. I was supposed to be fasting and praying to Allah for forgiveness for my sins—not committing more sins.

Ring! Ring!

I didn't recognize the number.

"Yes."

"Hello, is this Khadijah?"

"Yes, this is. Who's calling?"

"My boyfriend gave me your number. His name is Jaw."

"Jaw? I don't know a Jaw. I did give my number to a Brother L.J. at the beauty-supply store."

"My bad. That's his Muslim name. Family and close friends call him Jaw. I'm Sister Ja'ziya."

"It's a pleasure speaking to you. I'm new in the area."

"What brings you to Chicago? The city is nice, but not nice enough to visit in the summer time. This is the time of year when the murder rate is sky-high. I'm not trying to scare you."

Scare me? I guessed she ain't never been to Miami.

"Oh, I'm never scared. Have you ever heard of Little Haiti in Miami?"

"Yes, girl, I see that hood on the *First 48* all the time."

"That's exactly why I'm not scared of Chicago. I'm up here on a little family business. I could use a tour guide, if you are up to it?"

"I don't mind showing you around. I got a bad case of morning sickness, so mornings are never good for me. How about the weekend?"

"That's fine. We can attend Jumu'ah on Friday, if you are up to it?"

"Fine with me. See you Friday."

SIX

Bianca

"**W**ell I don't care how much it costs. I want Meek Mill at this party! Get it done, Manny."

Money was not an option. My daddy is filthy rich. Hello guys, my name is Bianca, but I prefer to be called Belle. I'm Black and Columbian. Yes, I know it's a very sexy combination. I'm fine as hell. I'm five foot even and I weigh 128 pounds. Yes, I'm thick in all the right places.

Pow! Pow!

I have brown curly hair that falls past my ass. I inherited my chinky eyes from my mom's side of the family. My mom is this little Black bombshell that caught my father's eye. She was visiting Columbia with her friends when she met my dad. I asked her what attracted her to him and she said, "I saw the power in his eyes."

My daddy is one of the most powerful men that walks the face of this earth. He has his hand in everything from politics to the drug game. Nobody messes with the Saldavar family and lives to tell that tale. My daddy taught me everything I know. So, when I told him I wanted him to supply my boyfriend, Young Meech, he agreed.

I love my man so much. I met him at a very dark time in his life. He was actually on the verge of committing suicide the night I accidently called him. I was trying to call Manny, but I ended up dialing him. After that night, he called me every day. We eventually started dating. He didn't act like he was sixteen. I was even more surprised and pleased to know that he had his own money. I think that's what attracted me to him. Now I see what my mother was talking about. I saw the power in his eyes. I not only saw it, but when I was in his presence, I also felt it.

And let me tell you, it feels good to be in the presence of a young boss in the making. You know every good thing don't last too long. Me and daddy hadn't been seeing eye to eye lately. He took a liking to Meech but started treating me different. I'd been meaning to call him and speak to him about how I've been feeling.

Where the hell is my phone?

"Hey, Daddy, what's going on?"

"You know I love you, right?"

"Yeah."

"Meech is great for business, but I don't think he's great for you."

Okay, so now he tells me how he really feels after five years.

"Where is all this coming from?"

"I know this life. You have been in this life for so long. Don't you want a normal life with a normal guy?"

"No! This is my life. You are the reason why this is my life. Now you want me to leave my man of five years and do something different?"

"Yes! Do as I say, not as I do. If you don't leave him, I will no longer supply him."

"What? How dare you."

"I'll cut you off as well."

I couldn't believe he was saying this to me. I loved my father dearly. I mean, this couldn't be happening. I held on to the phone without saying a word. I was trying to think of a solution. I came up with nothing. I loved my daddy. He was the number one man in my life.

"Hello? Bianca?"

"Yes, daddy, I'm here."

"What's it gonna be?"

"I love you, daddy."

"I love you too."

"I'm going to miss you."

Click!

I hung up on him with a heavy heart. I just cut off my father. I hope Meech don't get mad at me for this. I had to tell him. Tomorrow, he was supposed to re-up. I dialed his number.

"What's good, baby?"

"Um, are you busy? I need to talk to you."

"I'm free for you. What's wrong, pretty?"

"My daddy told me that if I didn't stop seeing you, he'd cut off your supply of dope and me as well."

"Damn, Pops tripping like that? I make that nigga tons of bread. So, what now? You done with me?"

I heard the hurt all in his voice. Of all people, Meech knew how much I loved and cherished my father. But what he didn't know is how much I loved and cherished him as well. The last five years of my life had been the best years of my life. No arguments, no other bitches, no bullshit. My daddy has lived his life. I was going to do the same.

"Hello, BeBe. Tell me something!"

"You gon' have to find you a new connect."

SEVEN

Young Meech

"**H**ey, Money Man, I need to holla at you and Outlaw ASAP!"

"I don't like the sound of this shit. Come get me. I'm at Mom Dukes house."

"I'm on my way."

I turned my radio on and zoned out.

"Look at all these young niggas flexin' from the bottom. We just want the money, the respect, and all the power."

That Meek Mill's check goes so hard. True shit though. Every time I get a break, it's always some nigga trying to throw a monkey wrench in my plans. I wasn't surprised that BeBe's dad wanted her to choose. To be honest with you, Columbians, Italians, Mexicans, and all the other different races don't like niggas. The men wanna fuck our beautiful black women, but they hate the men.

It fucked his head up that I brought him so much money. We never had a problem. I'm not about to dwell on it because he's not the only connect in the world. This just made me love my girl even more. Never in a million years did I think she would choose me over her father. I mean, I'm not a slouch. I got a lot of dough. My shit ain't as long as her pops's, but I can hold my own. There ain't nothing that she can't ask me for that I wouldn't get her. One thing about BeBe is she ain't lazy by a long shot. Her hustle game was just as hard as mine, if not harder. I think her father got mad because she no longer called him asking for money. She's my girl, and I told her that she didn't have to be on those streets. I got her. This was definitely a minor setback, but my comeback was going to be even harder. I pulled up to Heidi's crib that Jaw and Money Man bought her. This mutha was nice as hell. It kind of looked like the house from *The Fresh Prince of Bel-Air*.

Ding! Dong!

Outlaw came to the door.

"What up, boy?"

"Shit, come on. We're in the basement."

As soon as I stepped foot in the door, Heidi was coming down the stairs wearing all white. She had an unlit cigar in her mouth. This lady was a fool.

"Hey, Meech, welcome to the white house, baby."

"Oh yeah?"

I made a move, and she snapped.

"Uh-um, lil' boy. Take them shoes off before I punch you in the back of your damn head. Didn't I say welcome to the white house? Look around. Everything is white."

I looked around, and sure enough, everything was white.

"My bad, Heidi."

"My bad, my ass. Hurry up and take yo' ass downstairs with the rest of them dirty-ass lil' boys."

I looked at Outlaw, and he was cracking up. I shook my head and followed him to the basement.

"Dude, yo momma still crazy."

"You ain't know?"

The basement was totally different from upstairs. It was colorful as hell. The black leather sectional and the red-and-white throw rugs gave the room a relaxing feel. Money Man was sitting in front of the television playing the game. I sat next to him and took the lit blunt from the ash tray.

"We got a problem. BeBe's father gave her an ultimatum. Cut me off, or he's going to cut her off and quit supplying us."

Money Man paused the game and held his arms out toward me.

"Aw, baby, she broke up with you? Come give Money Man a hug."

"Fuck you, nigga! She chose me, fool."

He started cracking up.

"So, that means we are out of a connect then! Damn! She must really love yo' dirty ass to give up that million-dollar life."

"What we need to do is find another connect."

Money Man paused the game again and looked at Outlaw.

"Outlaw, tell Young what you been up to."

I pulled on the blunt and looked at Outlaw. This was going to be interesting.

"Remember a few weeks ago, I was telling you about them Haitian niggas?"

"Yeah."

"Well, the nigga known as Haiti Redd asked me if I wanted to make some extra bread. I told him yeah, and he put me down with him and his crew. I'm running one of his trap spots."

I didn't like where this was going.

"I been running his spot over there on 42nd and Calumet."

"Outlaw, what you doing, bruh?"

"Let me finish before you say anything. I got this. My plan is to gain his trust like I've been doing and then rob his ass blind."

"Who's supplying him?"

"His cousin that's still in Miami. They got a big connect down there. The work is some fire too. It's not that shit that he sold to the lil' niggas that were copping from me. The shit fire like the dope you get from BeBe's father. Listen, Meech, don't look at me like that. Dude thinks I'm some little-ass street punk trying to make a few dollars. He don't know about nothing we got going on over here. Let me find out who his connect's connect is."

"Man, this shit could blow up in our faces. We need a connect now though. Don't make me waste my money or some garbage."

Outlaw gave me a look that spoke volumes.

"Don't doubt me, Meech. I been loyal to you since day one. Once I find out what I need to know, I'ma send them goofy-ass niggas back to Miami in boxes."

Something in me felt like we were about to start another war. I was ready. I just hoped that this time we came out on top again.

EIGHT

JuJu

"Hey, Re. How's the Big Apple?"

"Girl, I'm so sick of all these snooty-ass white people. I can't wait to come home. I miss my city. Girl, you think Chicago got some big rats, wait 'til you see these New York rats. They some big ugly disrespectful muthafuckers. They'll walk past you and look you up and down like what?"

I started cracking up. I could just about imagine.

"Aw, Re, I miss you so much. This lil' girl is a hot-ass mess. Yesterday I caught her in my closet walking around in my heels. I melted when I looked in those pretty hazel eyes."

"You're a sucker! I don't be letting her run you, Ju. She's five years old, remember?"

"Girl, I'll do whatever I want with my niece."

"Okay, you say that shit now. Wait 'til she starts tearing your shit up. Don't call me."

"When are, you coming back? I'm so lonely."

"I'll be home soon. How is my baby in your belly doing?"

"Aw, he's fine. I'm tired of all the kicking he's been doing. The other day he kicked me so hard in my bladder that I peed."

"Did you tell Jaw it's a boy yet?"

"I'm waiting. He's been so busy lately. I'ma tell him soon."

I told her some more stuff and ended our call. I went into the next room to check on Tyshawn.

"Hey there, baby. You okay?"

She looked up at me with those pretty eyes and smiled.

"JuJu, when my momma coming back?"

"Soon, Pooh. Soon."

"Okay, you wanna watch a movie with me?"

I was so sleepy. All I wanted to do was crawl in my bed and shut my eyelids, but I couldn't tell that pretty face no.

"Yeah, baby. What you wanna watch?"

"*State Property.*"

"*STATE PROPERTY*? Girl, what the hell? Who let you watch that stuff?"

"Um, my daddy, Poohman."

"I'm going to have to have a talk with him. That's not a movie for a five-year-old little girl. Let's watch *Fast and Furious.*"

"Which one?"

"All of them!"

Three movies and two bowls of ice cream later, I finally had her little butt in the bed. She was a wonderful little girl with a sad past. She reminded me of her mother, JoJo, with her eyes, her little nose, and her long pretty hair. I hated the fact that she was related to Lil Man. I knew that one day we were going to have to see his face again. He was relentless, and I knew without a doubt that he was going to come for Tyshawn. Pregnant or not, I'd be ready. This time, one of us was going to send his ass to hell where he belonged.

Next Day

I really didn't want to go to Jumu'ah (prayer). It took everything in me not to call Khadijah and reschedule. When I got up, Jaw was already gone, and to my surprise, he took little Ms. Badass with him. I walked into the bathroom and turned on the shower. There was a Post-it note on the mirror that read, "I took Ty with me. Enjoy your day, my love."

That was so sweet. I called Khadijah to confirm our plans.

"As-Salaam-Alaikum."

"Wa-Alaikum-As-Salaam."

"I just called to let you know I was getting ready for Jumu'ah. Are you still coming?"

"Yes. What time should I pick you up?"

"It's 9:00 now. How about 11:00?"

"That's fine."

I gave her my address and then jumped in the shower. I was going to have my baby in just four short months. I couldn't wait.

Ring! Ring!

"I'm outside."

"Okay."

When I first saw her, I thought she looked evil. She had the darkest skin I had ever seen. She was completely covered up. I immediately put on my hijab to cover my hair. This was going to be an eventful day.

Khadijah

I ain't even been here that long, and I was sick and tired of this city. I missed Miami. I missed the action in Little Haiti. It was so boring up here. And they had the nerve to call this city "ChiRaq." Here I was on a blank mission to find a baby that I really didn't think existed. I didn't even have a clue what this mystery baby looked like. Ja'ziya was cool for the most part. I really didn't do females. They are all so dramatic, but I thought this might work though. She was sweet. At exactly 11:00 a.m. I was outside her condo on 68th and South Shore Dr.

I could see by just looking around the neighborhood that she might have a little money. The buildings were nice. The lake was a block away, and you could clearly see the downtown skyline. I bet that was a million-dollar view at night. When she finally appeared, she was cute as hell. I could tell she didn't know how to wear her hijab though. She had it wrapped around her head covering most of her face. I couldn't help but laugh. When she got in the car, I was still laughing.

"What you laughing at?"

"You. Why the hell are you wrapped up like a mummy?"

I laughed even harder.

"Don't laugh at me. I was trying to fix mine like yours."

"I don't cover my whole face. The only Muslims that do that, as far as I know, are the ones from the Middle East. Here, let me help you. Take it off."

When I got a look at her whole face, my heart started racing. I knew her face from somewhere. After a few seconds of nothing, it finally clicked. She was JuJu. She was the girl in the picture that D showed me. When I looked up, she was looking at me.

"Earth to Khadijah. Are you okay?"

"Yes, girl, I'm good. I was thinking about how to tie your hijab."

After I tied her hijab, we were off.

"You can take 69th to Stoney Island, and then take Stoney all the way to 73rd."

I didn't even wanna go pray now. I needed to call D Money and tell him about this. We arrived at the mosque in no time.

"Go ahead in there. I have to make a call."

"Oh, okay, hurry up. I don't wanna be by myself."

She got out of the car and was about to walk off, until I called her.

"JuJu!"

"Huh?"

"Smile!"

I took her picture with my phone.

"You are so pretty. I just had to take a picture."

"You are too sweet. Hurry up!"

I called my cousin.

"Yo! You got something for me?"

"Damn, no 'Hi! How are you?' nothing!"

"Hell naw, you find my baby?"

"I'm about to send you a picture. Call me back and tell me who it is."

I hung up and sent the picture. Not even ten seconds later and my phone was ringing.

"So, you found JuJu? How you do that? Never mind! It don't matter. Where is my baby?"

"I don't know. I haven't seen a little girl. I just met her today. Now that I know I'm on the right path, let me do me."

"I'm coming up there in a few days. I gotta meet with the connect, plus Haiti Redd said a few niggas want some—"

"I know what you mean! See you then."

"All right. Bye."

Damn! Maybe there was a baby out there after all. I felt it in my gut that there was about to be a lot of killings. I said a small prayer for my enemies.

"Yar-hamulkal lah!" (May Allah have mercy on you.)

NINE

Jaw

"Hey, you better sit down and put that seatbelt on before I spank yo' butt."

Damn, this lil' girl bad as hell.

"You not gon' spank me, Uncle Jaw. You gon' love me."

Now how could I spank her after she said that?

"Okay, I'm not gon' spank you, but sit down before you get us pulled over by the police."

"If they pull us over, I'ma tell them to get down or lay down, Uncle Jaw."

"You gon' tell them what? What the hell you been watching?"

"My daddy let me watch *State Property.*"

"Aw, naw. I'ma have a talk with him. Little girls shouldn't be watching stuff like that. You should be watching *The Lion King* or *Dora the Explorer.*"

"My daddy said cartoons are for pussies."

That nigga Poohman be tripping.

"You can't curse yet, Tyshawn. Pretty girls don't curse. Aren't you pretty?"

"Yes. Uncle Jaw."

"Then no cursing."

I took her to McDonald's and the mall for some light shopping. I had a ball with her. I couldn't wait 'til my baby came. I loved being a father.

Ring! Ring!

Even though I had fun, I was so glad to see JuJu calling.

"Hey, baby, where you at? This lil' girl crazy."

She started cracking up.

"I'm on my way back from the mosque. I decided to go to Jumu'ah with Khadijah."

"Oh yeah? Did you enjoy it?"

"It was different. I hope I can get used to it, Insha-Allah" (If Allah so wills.)

"Well, look at you. Subhaan-Allah (Glory to Allah). It's going to take some getting used to."

"I know, I know. Hey, I got a question. Did you tell Khadijah my name was JuJu?"

"I don't know. I probably did, why?"

"Nothing. I just asked. Where are you so I can come get my niece?"

"I'm taking this little thug to her daddy right now. Do you know she's been watching *State Property*?"

"I heard. I'm going to kill Poohman. Okay, I'm in the house. I love you."

It was time to re-up, so I decided to call my connect and set something up.

"Hola."

"What's going on, Papi?"

"Jaw, my man! How are you?"

"I'll be better when I see you. How about tomorrow?"

"You don't speak with Young Meech?"

"Not today. What's he got to do with me?"

"Ask him. I'm sorry, my friend. I will no longer supply you. Good luck."

Click!

What the fuck! I know Young Meech's ass ain't pissed this man off. Man, I'ma kill that fool. That was the best work we have ever got our hands on. I had to get down to the bottom of this shit. I called Young.

"What up, Jaw?"

"Shit, nigga, you tell me. I called the connect, and he said to ask you why he cut us off."

"Damn, that muthafucka's petty. He told BeBe that if she didn't leave me alone, he would cut me off. He cut her off too."

"You see, that's that bullshit. Now, what we gon' do?"

"Outlaw's working on something with those Haitians from Miami."

"Some Haitians? Is the work good?"

"Outlaw said it was. Come through. I'm 'bout to hang up."

I didn't like the sound of this shit, and I damn sho' didn't like the sound of dealing with some out-of-town dudes. I called Poohman.

"What up, bruh?"

"Meet me at Meech's crib."

"Here we go! Where my baby?"

"You mean, Ms. Get Down or Lay Down? She right here. Why you let her watch that bullshit?"

"I'm getting her ready."

"For what?"

"Life, nigga!"

Click!

TEN

Haiti Redd

"Hello?"

"What's going on over there?"

"Well, hello to you, my dear sister. I'm making progress. I'm actually about to put the lil' nigga Outlaw to the test."

"Aw hell naw. Not the test. What if he fails?"

"Then I keep looking for my next soldier. What about you? Did you find them hoes that D was talking about?"

"I actually found one of them. I don't think she is the one that has the girl, but I'm in the right spot."

"Good. Let me know if you need some assistance."

"Assistance? You know I can hold my own. Besides, the one I found don't even look like she 'bout that life. I really think D exaggerated about what he told us about these people. I spent all day with JuJu. She seems so clueless about the street life."

"Well let's show this city what Miami Haitians be about."

"Have you been to the mosque up here?"

"Now, dear brother, you know that if I don't do nothing else, I stay on my deen. I'll always put Allah first, no matter what I do."

"Just checking. Let me handle this business. I'll let you know the outcome."

After I hung up with my crazy-ass sister, I called my cousin, KeeKee. He had been real quiet lately.

"You ready?"

"Yup. I'm gon' wait 'til—"

"Don't wait for shit. Take Freddie, Blue Boy Black, and Gator with you. Make that shit quick."

"What if he recognizes me?"

"Does it matter? He's about to die anyway. Didn't you say you wanted to get shit cracking?"

"Yeah."

"Then go crack something."

I mean, how hard was it going to be to rob my own spot? I kind of felt bad that I was about to get the lil' nigga whacked. I had started to like him. Oh well. Fuck him! When you in these streets, things like this happen all the time. It's time to show these Chicago niggas that Miami boys are here to stay.

Outlaw

"A man gets the fuck in front of this house with all that noise."

"All right, Outlaw. Chill!"

Yeah, nigga! You know what time it is. I was tired of playing with all these punks over here. Little did they know they were about to wake up a sleeping giant.

Ring! Ring!

It was Haiti Redd.

"Yo, what up, boy?"

"Some of my homies 'bout to roll through."

"Well what they looking for?"

"Whatever it is, make sure you get my money first."

Click!

Make sure I get the money first? What type of shit he got going on? I had a bad feeling in my gut that told me what I already knew. This nigga was about to test my gangsta. Okay then, come on with it. I was about to murder me a nigga. I grabbed my phone and called my right-hand man.

"Outlaw, what it do, fool?"

"School Boy Slim, where you at? I think something about to pop off. I need you." .

"I'm wherever you need me to be."

I told him where I needed him to be and then I waited. I knew the nigga Haiti Redd was a clown. Clown niggas do stupid shit. Too bad for his homies he was sending over here. I was about to murk all of 'em!

School Boy Slim

I jumped up out of the pussy I was currently digging in and hopped in the shower. It'd been awhile since we had some excitement. I knew that Haiti Redd and his crew were going to be up to no good sooner or later. I definitely knew that if Khadijah showed up, shit was about of go from bad to terrible. Man, that bitch gave me nightmares. I met her ass my freshman year in college. We had a big-ass party on campus, and I was the go-to guy for the X pills. I had whatever pill you wanted: blue dolphins, green fishes, pink butterflies, red Louis Vuittons—everything! Anyway, I was posted up by the punch bowl when somebody walked up on me and grabbed my dick. I was shocked. These college hoes were freaky as hell.

"Damn, shorty, you know me like that to be grabbing my dick?"

"I'm trying to see how big it is before I let you fuck me."

Daammmnnn! She was bold. I didn't know whether to run or stay.

"So, what you think? Is it big enough?"

"Hell yeah, let's go!"

I shouldn't have never left with that ho. When we got back to the room, all hell broke loose. I ain't never had no pussy that good before in my life! I don't know what she did to me, but my dick would not go down for shit. I busted like four nuts, and my dick was still rock hard. We quickly became an item around school. I thought she was a sweet girl until I saw her cut a girl's face for grabbing my arm. After that it was like the devil came out. I didn't even know she

48

was Muslim. Don't get me wrong, I have absolutely no problems with Muslims. I don't think all of them are terrorists like that jackass Donald Trump.

She used to sit around me and chant shit in a different language that I didn't understand. If you asked me, I'd say the bitch was chanting some voodoo shit. After I told her that I didn't want to mess with her no more, my dick wouldn't get hard for like two months. My homie Blunt's grandma practiced that black magic shit. I had to go over there and let her break the spell that I know she put on me. Just thinking about the shit gave me the chills.

Ring! Ring!

"Yo, Outlaw, what's cracking?"

"You see that white Tahoe that just pulled up?"

"Yeah?"

"Get ready. I think this is them niggas that Haiti Redd sent over here."

"Well, I got you, bruh. Should I call—?"

"No! We got this. We don't need to involve Young or Money Man. They already think that me dealing with these goofies is a disaster waiting to happen."

"They're at the door."

ELEVEN

Money Man

I needed to unwind, so I hit the strip club right off 115th. I was gonna be cheap and hit up Arnie's in Harvey, but them hoes stank. Us not having a connect was fucking with my mental. We couldn't be kings of the city if we couldn't supply the work.

"You want a dance?"

I was so deep in my thoughts that I never saw her approach me. She was bad as hell.

"Goddamn, girl!"

She was a cute lil' redbone with some pretty-ass teeth. Shorty was thick to death. Her booty was so big that my dick almost jumped through my pants.

"Yeah, you can give a dance."

As soon as she stood in front of me, the song "Body Party" by Ciara came on.

"My body is your party, baby; nobody's invited but you, baby."

She turned around and looked me dead in my eyes. I had a clear view of that pretty-ass pussy. *Damn! I think I'm in love.* When the song was over, she sat on my lap and whispered in my ear.

"My name is TaTa-lalicious."

I was about to tell her my name, but she put her finger up to my mouth and shushed me.

"I know who you are. You Money Man. I love your mixtapes."

I ain't gon' lie. I poked my chest out some. Shorty made a nigga feel real good. My music was my baby. I slang dope for the money. My music gives me life for real.

"What time you get off?"

"In twenty minutes. I'm riding with you?"

"Hell yeah. I'ma be in the parking lot. I'm driving a—"

"The black two-door Benz."

I cracked a smile. Yeah, these hoes know who the fuck I am. I'm that nigga without a doubt. I was in the car waiting on shorty when my phone rang.

"What up, Meech?"

"Chilling. Where you at?"

"'Bout to leave the strip club and smash this bitch named TaTa-la something."

"TaTa-lalicious? She light-skinned and thick as hell?"

"That's the one."

"Bruh, be careful with that one. Remember when Fat Boy got killed at the Ramada Inn?"

"Yeah, I remember that bullshit."

"Word around town is that she had something to do with it. She set him up."

"Oh, I'm not worried about that. I'll murk this bitch quick, fast, and in a hurry."

"Just be careful, my dude. These hoes ain't loyal."

"One."

It's a damn shame you can't trust a bitch nowadays. I watched her strut across the parking lot like she was a top model. I was slopping. I had to hurry up and close my mouth.

"You with me the whole night?"

She reached across the armrest and grabbed a handful of dick.

"Does that answer your question?"

I turned up my radio and sped out of the parking lot. I hit the gas station on 111th. I needed to gas up. I know the jack boys (robbers) be out this time of the night. They could try and run up on me if they wanted to. The police station was right next door. After I paid, I was walking toward my car when I saw something suspicious. I put it in the back of my mind for now and pumped my gas. I hit the expressway doing seventy. I love foreign cars. The ride was so smooth.

"What hotel we going to?"

I turned the music down and looked at her.

"Why?"

I didn't mean for it to come out harsh, but fuck it. It is what it is.

"I was just asking."

I ignored her and turned my music back up. Out of the corner of my eye I saw that her phone kept lighting up. She was texting somebody. Now I started thinking about what Young had just told me. Then I thought about what I saw when I was walking out of the gas station. She was talking on her phone, but when she saw me she quickly hung up. Was this bitch really that dumb? I was about to pull her card.

"We 'bout to hit the Baymont on Sibley. Is that cool?"

"That's fine, baby."

I picked up my phone like I was 'bout to make a call. I wanted her to think I wasn't paying her ass no attention. Not even twenty seconds later she started typing on her phone. *Oh yeah?* Young was right. This slut was trying to set me up. I got off of the expressway on Sibley and drove right past the hotel. Just like I expected, she looked at me.

"You passed the hotel."

"I changed my mind. We going to the Days Inn. Is that alright with you?"

What she didn't know was that the Days Inn was a low-key hotel with no camera. I had to kill this ho for even trying to play me like I was a chump-ass nigga. I didn't even want the pussy no more.

"Hey, suck my dick."

She looked a little surprised by my request.

"Baby, as soon as we get in the room I'm going to take good care of you."

She had the nerve to lick her lips and rub my dick. If that was her way of trying to seduce me, the bitch failed. She should have tried something else.

"Naw, you can suck my shit right now. Yo' head might be garbage anyway. Let me see."

"Aw, baby, ain't shit garbage about me."

I must have pushed some buttons. She snatched my dick out of my pants and wrapped her lips around it, applying just the right amount of pressure. Up and down she went, round and round, rotating her tongue around the tip of my dick. She softly kissed the tip of my dick. Damn, she was raw with her shit. Too bad my dick was going to be the last dick she ever sucked. The head was so good that I hit a pothole coming in the parking lot.

"Go get the room."

I guess she enjoyed sucking my dick. Stupid-ass bitch left her phone when she got out of the car. I grabbed it and went straight to the text messages. This ol' musty-ass bitch was telling some nigga named Lucky that she had a sweet lick. He texted her back and reminded her that she knew just what to do. It went on and on about what hotel we were going to be at and shit. My trigger finger started itching. She got back in the car, and I handed her the phone. The look in her eyes told me what I already knew. She was busted.

"Y'all hoes ain't shit. What you think? You was going to do me like Fat Boy?"

I guess when you're faced with a life-or-death situation, you'll do anything to survive. She whipped out a big-ass knife.

"Nigga, you know what time it is? Run them pockets!"

I almost laughed in her face. Ol' fake-ass gangsta. But I was going to show her that I was a true muthafucking G. She dialed a number on her phone.

"We at the Days Inn, baby."

I didn't even give her a chance to finish her statement.

Boom!

I blew her brains all over my passenger side window. I opened the door and kicked her ass out of my car, but not before grabbing her phone out of her hands.

"Hello! TaTa? TaTa? Say something."

"Come pick up this bitch and her brains up out of the parking lot of the Days Inn Hotel in Lansing."

"Who the fuck is this?"

"The wrong nigga!"

I pulled out of the parking lot and went across the street to the twenty-four-hour car wash. My luck with hoes was terrible.

I'ma find Mrs. Right one day. Maybe I need to go to church.

TWELVE

Khadijah

I had been on to JuJu like a fly to fresh shit. We went everywhere together. I still hadn't seen no damn baby. I was starting to think what I always thought: there was no baby. I was chilling at JuJu's crib with her one day, when her phone rang.

"Hello? What do you mean pick her up? She was fighting? I'm on my way."

She got up off of the couch and wobbled her big ass into her bedroom. I didn't want to be nosey, but I asked anyway.

"Girl, who was fighting?"

She came out fully dressed.

"My niece. I gotta go get her from daycare. She was fighting."

"Your niece? How old is she?"

"She's five going on fifty."

"Well if you don't mind me asking, where is her mother?"

She shook her head and exhaled.

"It's a long story. Her mother was killed by her father when she was a few weeks old. My best friend, ReRe, was the one watching her when it all happened. With the help of

Jaw's Auntie ReRe and her boyfriend, Poohman, she was able to get full custody of her. ReRe is in New York right now on business. Poohman is Jaw's best friend. He sees her, but he's doing what he needs to do to keep food on the table. I'ma beat her ass, I swear."

I had to hide the excitement on my face.

"They was so nice to take her in. What's her name?"

"Tyshawn Christina. Come on, you wanna ride with me?"

"Of course."

I was going to wait and call D. I wanted to make sure this little girl was, in fact, his baby. About twenty minutes later we pulled up to the daycare. There were kids everywhere. Lord knows I hate kids. All they wanna do is eat candy and bounce around all damn day. I sure don't have a problem punching their asses in the throat or the stomach.

When JuJu came walking out with Tyshawn, I almost fainted. She was a pretty little girl. I had to hurry up and snap a picture of them so I could send it to my cousin. She had some thick, curly hair that sat in a puffy ponytail at the top of her head. When they got in the car, I was able to get a better look at her. Damn! This was his baby. She had the prettiest hazel eyes I had ever seen. I'm sure those came from her mother's side, but she had his face, his nose, and—oh my star—his mouth.

"Say hi, Tyshawn."

She looked at me with the weirdest look and rolled her eyes. I started cracking up. JuJu wasn't having it.

"Little girl, I am two seconds from whooping your ass. I don't know what has gotten into you, but I'm going to beat it out. Get your life before I get it for you."

"It's cool, JuJu."

"No it's not. She is a child, and she's going to act like it around me."

Tyshawn looked at me and put her hand to her head and twirled it around. She was secretly telling me JuJu was crazy. I started laughing again.

"What's your name?"

"Khadijah. What's yours?"

"You already know my name. Where you from?"

"Miami."

"I wanna go to Miami. They got a lot of nice people down there."

"How do you know if you ain't never been there?"

"Well, my daddy goes to Miami all the time to meet my Uncle Sal. He said Sal got that work for the low—"

"TYSHAWN! Shut up right now. I don't know what the hell is wrong with you. Khadijah, you have to excuse her, please. She don't act like this on a regular basis."

Oh weeee! This little girl is bad as hell. She got a mouth on her. I wonder what else she'll tell me if we were alone. I was going to try and make that happen.

58

THIRTEEN

Outlaw

Knock! Knock!
I checked my gun to make sure the safety was off. I don't know how that nigga, Haiti Redd, runs shit in Miami, but up here in the Chi we don't play about our money. I got me fucked up if he thought that I was going to let his friends punk me. I opened the door like I was expecting them.

"What up?"

"You Outlaw?"

"What you need?"

"Haiti Redd sent me over here to get three bricks. Hook me up."

Now see, there goes that bullshit right there. We all know in the drug game that asking for a hookup means you want something extra without paying for it. I don't do hookups. Come with all my money or get the fuck on. I might pop yo' ass for wasting my time.

"Come in."

I stepped to the side to let him in. I stopped his buddies at the door.

"It don't take three of y'all to cop no work."

I knew what the fuck this was. How you come to cop three bricks with no money bag? That was another red flag.

"How the fuck you walk up in here asking for three bricks and you ain't got no money bag in your hands?"

The one I let in quickly upped his banger on me.

"Fuck all that talking shit! Let me get the work and all the money I know y'all niggas over here are holding."

I chuckled a little because I had known it. I looked at him and shook my head.

"What the fuck's so funny, nigga? This a robbery, bitch. Give it up before I blast yo' ass."

I held my breath and waited for School Boy Slim to come through for a nigga. If I reached for my pistol, he would surely shoot me. *Come on, Slim. Where you at, boy?*

School Boy Slim

After I hung with Outlaw, I got ready for action. I had to be on point. I didn't think shit was going to go wrong, until I saw one of them niggas pull out his gun.

"Aw hell! Yeah, here we go, boy."

Click! Clack!

Renting this crib right across the street from Outlaw's trap spot was a great idea. I zoomed in on my target and pulled the trigger.

Outlaw

I closed my eyes and said a quick prayer, but my prayer was interrupted when I felt something spray on my face.

"Aw shit."

One of them niggas screamed. When I opened my eyes, I jumped back. Half of his muthafucking head was missing. All right, my nigga Slim. I quickly followed suit and pulled out my Glock .40. I shot the dude that was closest to me between his eyes. He stared at me until he dropped to the floor. The third dude took off running through the house to the back door. I was hot on his tail.

"Umm, bitch-ass nigga. Where you think, you going?"

Boc!

I shot him in the back as he was trying to run out of the back door.

"ARRGGHHH. Please don't kill me."

"Nigga, don't beg. Who put you up to this?"

"Please don't—!"

"Tell me what I wanna know."

WHACK!

I slapped the shit out of his scary ass.

"Haiti Redd told us to come punk you. He said that you was a lil' nigga and he didn't think you could hold your own."

Punk me? Really now!

"He wanted us to rob you and see if you would—"

Boc! Boc! Boc!

I didn't wanna hear anything else. Nigga wanted to test me? That nigga done lost his mind. I ran back to the front of the house and looked out the window to see if anybody was out there being nosey. There wasn't a soul in sight. Damn shame how when shots are fired in the city, people go on about their business like it's normal. I hit Slim's phone.

"Good shot, boy."

"You good?"

"Hell yeah. Pull around the back so I can get all this dope and money out of here. I don't know why that nigga chose to send them goofies to his most profitable spot. I'm 'bout to take all his shit now."

"Who was them niggas?"

"Some clowns that Haiti Redd sent over here to test my gangsta."

"Hell naw. He gon' be hot as fish grease once he sees that mess over there."

"Fuck that bum. It's time to show him who I really am."

I went to the stash spot and grabbed everything. This was his most lucrative spot. Why send them niggas over here? I could tell he wasn't as smart as he portrayed. *I'ma take all the money and dope for my pain and suffering.* After I loaded up all the money and dope, I made another call.

"Outlaw, what's good boy?"

He sounded a little surprised to hear from me.

"Since you like testing people, I'ma show you my true colors. You got me fucked up, pussy."

"Whoa, lil' nigga! What are you talking about?"

"Act stupid all you want. I'ma see yo' ass in traffic. You might wanna send the coroner over here to scrape ya boys' brains up off of the floor."

Click!

There was war on them Miami niggas. I was ready to get back to doing what I loved doing the most. Killing!

FOURTEEN

Young Meech

Today was my twenty-first birthday. I felt old as hell. My life has been nothing but normal. Tonight, was my birthday party, and I couldn't say that I was looking forward to it. I was in the wrong business to be all out in the limelight, but I promised my girl I would let her throw me a big party.

"Baby, I'm about to go to the mall real quick. I forgot to grab something."

"Girl, why you didn't get all of your stuff when you went the first time? You need to hurry up so we can get ready. I'm trying to be out of this house at nine thirty. Don't be all day."

She walked over to me and gave me a kiss on my lips.

"I won't be long."

As soon as she walked out the door, I lay down. I was about to try and get a lil' nap in, but as soon as I closed my eyes, my damn phone rang.

"What up?"

"Damn, nigga! You good?"

"I was trying to take a nap until you called. What you want?"

"A nap? Nigga, you ain't in kindergarten! Get yo' ass up. I'm about to come get you."

"Hell naw, Money Man! I'm sleepy."

"Outlaw and Slim just laid a few of them Miami boys down."

Damn! I knew there was going to be some shit dealing with them cats.

"Come get me."

"I'm outside already."

"Yo' stalking ass."

"Come on out here, birthday boy, so I can give you your birthday licks."

"Nigga, if you hit me, we fighting."

As soon as I jumped in the car and seen his face, I knew that there was about to be a serious war.

"What happened?"

"To make a long story short, the boy named Haiti Redd tried to send some dudes to rob Outlaw."

"Aw, why he do that?"

"He not only killed the dudes, but he took all the work and money that was in the house."

I started cracking up because Outlaw was serious. That boy there was certified.

"So now we got beef, right?"

"Pretty much."

"Damn, joe! I told him the shit wasn't worth it. He had some good-ass work, but now look."

"School Boy helped him."

"Them two little muthafuckas gon' give me gray hairs."

He started laughing at me. I didn't think that shit was funny at all.

"You talking about them gon' give you gray hair."

"So."

"Nigga, you're getting old. That's where the gray hair is coming from. Don't blame it on them."

"Man, shut up! Who you bring to my party?"

"Heidi."

"Aw hell, Money Man. You better make sure she stays on her best fucking behavior."

"Yeah right. You know better. Is Lil Mama coming?"

"She said she was. I can't wait to see her. She's been in Paris the majority of the summer."

"Anybody hear from Boo?"

"Last I heard, she and Lil Mama fell out because Boo got mad about some petty shit."

"Boo's ass been on some bullshit lately though."

"Oh well, fuck her. I'm 'bout to go up in here and get ready for my party. Get there on time, boy."

I got out of the car and started walking upstairs, when something told me to look to my right. I saw a black Tahoe with its windows tinted. It pulled off from the parking lot up the street and was slowly creeping my way. I couldn't see who was in there, but I felt that whoever was in there was looking right at me. *Yeah, all right. Let a muthafucka act up tonight. I'ma fuck around and blow them candles out.*

BeBe

"I don't like sneaking around behind his back, Manny, but he won't talk to me."

"If your father finds out that I'm selling you product behind his back, you know I'm a dead man, right?"

"I know, Manny, thank you."

"Why don't you leave him and just come home?"

"Because I love him, Manny. He is everything I want, but he's everything Daddy hates. You know Daddy don't want no nigga to rise to the top. Meech made him a lot of money. I feel like he was threatened by his hustle."

"You are right. He don't want nobody to be anywhere close to his status. You know I got you, BeBe. Just be careful, and call your mom. She misses you."

I felt like there was something he wasn't telling me.

"Manny, what's on your mind?"

"Your father has been in contact with some very dangerous people from Miami."

"And?"

"Well let's just say that you and your boyfriend's crew needs to watch y'all's back."

"Okay. As long as you keep supplying me, I'm good."

A girl's gotta do what a girl's gotta do. The work Meech was getting from them Haitians was stepped on, and he knew it. In order for my man to run a foolproof enterprise, he had to have the best product. Now that that was out of the way, I was going to hit the mall real quick. I had to hurry up and get back before he started calling my phone. He was going to love the party I planned for him. Well, I hoped so.

Outlaw

"Hey, let me get them in at nine o'clock."

Tonight was Young's party, so you know we had to show up and shut shit down. Me and Slim hit the mall for some last-minute shopping.

"Man, Outlaw, you know how many hoes gon' be at this party tonight? I'm fucking somebody's bitch tonight."

"You dumb as hell. Let's hit the jewelry store real quick. I want a watch."

We paid for our shoes and headed to the jewelry store. I had a fetish for watches. I wanted something that was going to make the hoes slob. I grabbed the door to the store and was about to pull it, just as Slim grabbed my arm.

"Man, hell naw! There goes Haiti Redd's sister. Remember the bitch I was telling you put a spell on my dick? That's her. What the fuck is she doing up here? Man, something ain't right, Outlaw. It's one thing to have her brother up here trying to make some money, but her? She's looking for something or somebody. Let's get the fuck out of here before she sees me."

I ain't never seen my boy that spooked before. The shit kinda made me mad. *Tonight, better go off without a hitch. I'm not playing. Somebody gon' die if it don't!*

FIFTEEN

Khadijah

I couldn't believe I found D's daughter. When I sent him the picture, he called me back ASAP.

"I'm on the next flight up there. Don't lose her."

"I'm on it. Check this out though. It's going to be hard to get her by herself."

"Then kill everybody around. What's so hard about that? By any means necessary, remember?"

"I got you."

That boy was retarded. Why kill people when I didn't have to. I was a goon, but I was far from a monster!

Ring! Ring!

It was D again.

"What?"

"Don't what me, bitch! Did you get the bracelet made?"

"I'm up here at the mall right now."

"When you pick it up, make sure they wrap it up real pretty."

"I know, D. You don't have to keep repeating shit to me. I'm not slow like you all is."

He started giggling.

"Yo' momma slow, bitch. Quit insulting me. I'm sensitive. I can't wait to see her."

"I'm about to walk in the store. Let me call you back."

I made my way to Zale's jewelry store to pick up the bracelet he ordered for her. Personally I didn't think a five-year-old needed a $20,000 bracelet, but what the hell did I know?

"Hello. I'm here to pick up a bracelet ordered by Derrick Walker."

The sales clerk typed in some information.

"Would you be paying for that in credit?"

I pulled out a wad of cash.

"No. Cash."

JuJu

"Jaw, I put your clothes on the bed."

I was mad I had to miss Young's twenty-first birthday party. I could have gone, but I'm big as hell. Plus, my besties are both in different parts of the world. I didn't want to go without them.

"Baby, you seen my Gucci belt?"

"Your belt is in the closet. Look for it."

I walked in the room and just stared at my man. Damn, he was fine as hell. I had just finished twisting his dreads, so his hair was on point. He stood in the closet shifting through some belts in nothing but his Calvin Klein boxer briefs. I was too far along to have some back-creaking sex. I'd fuck around and have to be rushed to the hospital. Fuck it. I was so horny. I was about to take that chance. When I looked up, I caught him staring at me. Busted!

"Why you over there looking at me like I'm a T-bone steak?"

"Hurry up and give me some. You gotta be quiet because our nosey-ass niece is in the next room."

As soon as I took my gown off, Ms. Badass came in and killed my vibe. Damn!

"TeTe, what y'all doing?"

I rolled my eyes and went back into the living room. About twenty minutes later Jaw came out of the room looking like a GQ model.

I guess Tyshawn read my mind.

"Uncle Jaw, you look like a model."

He smiled. I had to admit it. He was looking damn good.

"Don't make me crash the party and beat a bitch down."

He smiled that sexy-ass smile. Oh my stars, my panties got soaked. He came and kissed my forehead.

"You don't have too much fat, girl. All this chocolate is yours."

Before I could respond, Tyshawn's lil' grown ass jumped in.

"What party? I wanna go. Come on, TeTe, let's hit the Quan on them hoes."

Jaw started cracking up. I didn't laugh because I didn't think it was funny.

"You better watch your mouth before I pop you in it."

Jaw checked his watch.

"I gotta go grab Poohman, baby."

"Tell him we are going to have a long talk about this lil' girl."

After Jaw left, we climbed on the couch and fell asleep. I hoped my son didn't act like her bad ass.

Khadijah

I stood in the mirror admiring the body Allah blessed me with. At five foot six I was stacked, and I knew it. I had some perky-ass 36 Ds and a twenty-seven-inch waist. My hips were forty-two inches. Yes, I was that bitch. Too bad I kept it all covered up under all my loose-fitting clothes. On special occasions I would let it all hang out. You know, catch a nigga's eye and reel him in. Tonight was somebody named Young Meech's birthday party. The whole crew was going to go check out the city's biggest competition. D's plane landed about an hour ago, but he didn't want me to pick him up from the airport. He came and grabbed the bracelet and bounced. Tonight I was going to enjoy myself. I was going to dance all night long and forget about the trouble that we were about to cause in this city.

Ring! Ring!

Who the fuck was disturbing me from getting ready? I was trying to have some much-needed me time. It was JuJu.

"Hey, fat mama. What you doing?"

"Laying on my couch 'bout to fall back to sleep. I'm bored. You wanna come over?"

"Sorry, toots. I'm actually about to go to a party."

"A party? You?"

"I know, right? My cousin flew in from out of town, so we are about to go out and chill and turn up."

"Damn, I wish I could go. I don't have a babysitter to watch little Ms. Badass. Have fun for me too."

"Okay, girl, good night."

I almost felt bad for what was in store for her. Almost! Business is business. *Let me get my ass on out of here.* I looked in the mirror one last time and blew myself a kiss. I had on a red Gucci romper that showed all this thickness. My dreads were freshly twisted, and my makeup was flawless. It was time for me to show the world the other me.

SIXTEEN

D Money

"**W**ell, what the fuck you think I'ma do?"
"Now that you know where she is, just do what you gotta do. When you ready, go get her."

"What time are you going to the party?"

"Now."

"Meet me at the front door. Let's crash that bitch in style."

I hung up the phone and got my thoughts together. I came back to Chicago to get my revenge! Lil Man died a long time ago. Call me D Money. I went to Miami after I killed the mother of my child. The bitch tried to set me up, so she had to go. The Eastside Crazy Crew might have thought they scared me out of town, but they didn't. I'm not scared of shit but my own shadow. I had to leave. I was tired of losing to them. I had to get my mind right and my weight up. It was hard leaving the city without my baby. But after five years I was ready. I'm that nigga. I run Miami. I linked up with my cousin, Haiti Redd, and the rest is history. I know how to kill, but Haiti Redd taught me how to hustle. He showed me how to survive. I'm home now, and I plan to kill every muthafucker that gets in my way. After I wiped out Young

Meech and his little crew, I was going to get my daughter. *Daddy's home!*

Young Meech

"Man, shorty. Let's go!"

"I'm coming, baby."

Damn! I hate waiting on females. Tonight, was my night. I just wanted to party and relax. I can't even front. I've been looking forward to this lil' party. The big twenty-one. I was fresh to death tonight. I had on some True Religion shorts and a white True Religion button-up. See, I'm simple. Nothing too flashy. My wrist shined, my neck was winged out, and my ears sparkled. I had on just enough ice to show the city that I was the king. My girl came downstairs making me stare a little bit longer than I intended to. She had on an all-white David Koma mini dress with some gold Gucci heels that laced up her legs. I prayed that I didn't have to fuck nobody up tonight.

About forty-five minutes later we walked in Adriana's to a packed club. The DJ was playing my shit, "Sleeping on the Floor," by Lil Bibby:

That .40 got a drum, bitch. I feel like Nick Cannon, ay.
Raised in the slums so you know I'm still damaged, ay.
Told her let me fuck, ho you know I'm real mannish.

"Aw shit! That nigga Young Meech and them Chi City Boys are in the building. Show my boy some love. Happy birthday, King Meech."

I instantly wanted to correct him. King was my father. My girl squeezed my arm and whispered in my ear.

"Relax, baby. You are my king. The streets love you. Let them love you."

I nodded my head and made my way to the VIP area reserved for us. As soon as I hit the VIP area, I saw Heidi dropping it like it was hot on the dance floor. I started cracking up when I saw that shit. I searched the scene for Money Man. When I saw him, he was in the corner shaking his head. He looked up and smiled when he saw me.

"Man, you see yo momma dropping it low on the dance floor?"

"I can't do shit with that lady. I see I'ma have to fuck one of these lil' niggas up though for dancing all over her."

"I can't take it."

I grabbed one of the many bottles of Moet we had and poured me a glass. The DJ turned the music off.

"What the fuck?"

"Everybody, welcome Chicago's finest, Lil Durk, to the stage."

Lil Durk hit the stage and turned the fuck up.

"Before I tear this muthafucking roof off of the club, I wanna say Happy Birthday to that nigga, King Meech."

After Lil Durk killed it, I thought it was over 'til Meek Mill hopped on the stage and did his thang:

Oh, I been that nigga fo' the money and fame.

I been that nigga fo' da diamonds and chain.

I been that nigga fo' the phones and the clothes.

I had my hands in the air repping my city. The whole club was on fire. My girl was in front of me dropping her ass like a true stripper. I instantly looked around to see what niggas was staring. All the niggas in the section I was in were drooling. The club erupted when Rick Ross hit the stage. I almost spit my drink out when Heidi's ass tried to jump on the stage.

"Money Man, go get yo momma, dude."

I fell out laughing when he grabbed her and walked her back to the VIP area.

"Money Man, I don't know why the fuck you grabbed me. I know you gon' let me show him what a real bitch looks like. He winked at me."

"Ma, no he didn't."

"Yes he did."

"Man, ma, you almost got put out the club. You can't be jumping on the stage trying to grab that man. Stay right here!"

My party was in full swing. Everybody was having a good time. Too bad the fun didn't last that long.

Haiti Redd

"What's good, D? Glad you finally decided to join us. You ready?"

We were outside of the club waiting for Khadijah's slow ass to pull up. When she stepped out of the car, I wanted to send her ass back home.

"What the fuck you got on?"

"Don't get mad at me 'cause I'm looking like a bag of money."

We had some of our crew go in already so we didn't look all suspicious. Our crew was everywhere. I had niggas on the dance floor, at the bar, and standing on the wall. There were also naked hoes everywhere. Goddamn!

Outlaw

I was actually having a good time. Aside from my momma trying to jump on the stage with Rick Ross, everything was a'ight until I saw that nigga Haiti Redd walk in the door. I grabbed Young Meech by the arm and tapped Money Man on his shoulder.

"Hey, that nigga Haiti Redd just walked up in here."

Young Meech scanned the crowd, and when he spotted Haiti Redd, he shook his head like he was seeing spots or something.

"Young, what?"

"Lil Man."

School Boy Slim

I knew I was fucking somebody's ho tonight. I had a gang of hoes on my dick. *Hello!* The party was juking. I had to piss, so I headed for the restroom. Somebody walked up on me from behind and grabbed my dick. When I turned around I almost pissed on myself.

"What's good, baby? You miss me?"

There weren't too many things in the world that I was scared of. This bitch was definitely one on that list.

"Man, what the fuck you on? Let my dick go."

"You still mad about that spell I put on you?"

"You a crazy bitch. Stay the fuck away from me before I shoot you in the face." Instead of going to the restroom, I went straight to the VIP area to tell my crew what was going on. I wasn't the only one on high alert. Young Meech had his eye locked on something or should I say someone in the crowd.

"Young, we got problems."

"We sure do."

"The bitch that put that spell on me is here."

"Lil Man is here, too."

Jaw

The party was in full swing once Young Meech made his appearance. I was hyped when Lil Durk, Meek Mill, and Rick Ross hit the stage. Me and Poohman were chilling in the cut and getting fucked up, when I felt some bad-ass energy invade my senses. Poohman must have felt it too, because he stood up and tapped my shoulder.

"Why yo' brothers and Young Meech up there looking like that?"

From where we sat we had a great view of the VIP area. They were all looking at something. I followed their eyes. When I saw what they were looking at, my heart starting beating fast as hell.

"Lil Man! It can't be!"

Lil Man was with a nigga with fire-engine-red dreads. Was that the Miami nigga who Outlaw was talking about?

"Come on, Poohman. There's about to be some shit."

I heard a nigga calling my name. I turned around to see my boy Gutta coming toward me. I turned to holler at him, all while keeping my eyes on them Miami niggas.

"What up, Jaw? Let me holla at you. Me and my girl were over there at the bar, and I heard some niggas talking about taking down them Chi City Boys. I know that's Young Meech and your little brothers."

"Oh yeah? Where they at?"

He pointed to the bar.

"You know we go way back. I'm riding. What you trying to do?"

"You know what we 'bout to do. Let me get my momma up out of here. You should send your girl home because we 'bout to send this bitch up."

"Hell naw. My girl's staying. Shorty got a mean pistol game. Shit, she one of them country-thick white broads. She taught me how to shoot. We'll be outside."

I headed to the VIP area looking for Heidi. I wished Money Man would have just sent her home instead of talking in front of her, because now she was talking bullshit.

"Where them niggas at? You know Heidi D ain't never scared."

I shook my head.

"Young Meech? You know that nigga Lil Man is up in here?"

"I know, I saw him. He got some niggas up in here with him too. We 'bout to get up out of here. If they follow us, then we gon' take it to the streets."

"Let's go."

We got all of our shit and made our way through the crowd. I thought I saw a familiar face, but I wasn't sure. I was slapped. I could barely stand up. Where did I know that face from? She was a bold bitch too. She walked straight up to School Boy and blew him a kiss. Slim looked spooked.

"Man! Bitch, get the fuck out of my face."

She smiled at him a focused her attention on Money Man.

"So, what's your name?"

Before he could respond, Heidi stepped up.

"Uh-uh, bitch. Back up off my son, ho, before I drop yo' ass. You just blew a kiss to his friend, and now you in his face? Move around lil' girl."

"Your son? What the fuck is an old lady like you doing in the club? You should be home doing crossword puzzles or something. Old bitch!"

I tried to grab her, but I was too slow.

Wham!

"I got your old bitch."

Crack!

My momma kicked it off. Next thing you know bottles started flying and bitches started screaming. It was a total disaster. Everybody split up.

"Come on, Poohman. We gotta get up out of here."

Young Meech

After Heidi hit that girl, all hell broke loose. I grabbed my girl's hand and ran for the exit. I wasn't running; I was trying to get my girl to safety. When we got outside, I threw her the car keys.

"Go home!"

"What about you?"

"I'm good. Go!"

I reached in the car and grabbed my .45 out of the stash spot.

"Young, turn around!" Outlaw yelled out.

When I did, I was staring down the barrel of a sawed-off shotgun.

"Hello Young, my buddy. Ain't it a nice night to die? You ready?"

My crew was all scattered out all over the parking lot. Outlaw was the closest, but he was engaged in a gun battle himself.

Pop!

I saw the nigga who Outlaw was shooting it out with fall to the ground. Lil Man's giggling brought me back to reality. We stared each other down for a few seconds.

"Pull the trigger, nigga. I ain't never scared."

I meant that. I was done being through so much bullshit that death didn't scare me.

"Oh, so you think you tough?"

Click! Clack!

"Die then!"

Boom! Boom!

I dropped to my knees thinking that my life was over. He hit me in my chest, but I had on my trusty Kevlar vest.

"Baby, get up. Let's go."

I was so happy to see her face.

"Damn, I see your aim is still on point."

"Come on, son. Get in the car."

I got in her car, and we sped off.

"Meech! Take off the vest. Are you hit?"

I unstrapped the vest and felt around my chest, which was on fire.

"Naw, I'm not hit. Where the hell you come from?"

"I was pulling up into the parking lot when I saw all of y'all running out of the club. Who was that I shot?"

"Lil Man."

"Lil Man? Aw fuck! Call up everybody to see if they are okay. There's about to be some shit."

SEVENTEEN

JuJu

Jaw finally walked through the door after 4:00 a.m. I lay in the bed for a few minutes and just watched his movements. He seemed aggravated about something.

"Baby, what's wrong with you?"

He came and sat down on the bed.

"He's back."

"Who?"

"Lil Man."

I sat up in bed and had to take a sip of my water. Did I hear him right?

"Lil Man is back here? In Chicago?"

"I think he's back for Tyshawn."

"Well he's going to die trying to get her. Does he know we have her?"

"I don't think he does. He showed up at the club last night. He looked the same, but he's matured some. He didn't even start shit last night. Heidi did."

"Oh Lord, what she do?"

"She hit the bitch that came with them. The shit spilled out into the parking lot. Me and Poohman took Heidi and dipped."

"I gotta call Re. She needs to—"

"To stay her ass in New York. We got this. Don't call her, Ju. Don't call Dirt neither."

"Okay, now you say don't call them, but if anything happens—!"

"Ain't shit gon' happen."

I got up out of bed to go check on Tyshawn. She was curled up in her bed asleep. I knew that one day he would come back for her. I just wished it wasn't at a time like this. I was pregnant. I couldn't do shit without risking my baby's life. I kissed Tyshawn and went back in the room. Jaw was lying in the bed channel surfing.

"You better make sure he doesn't come for her."

He turned the television off and looked at me.

"Baby, there ain't a doubt in my mind that he's coming for her."

I started to cry. My hormones were all jacked up.

"What are we going to do?"

"We gon' do what we do best. Win!"

Lil Mama

I couldn't sleep after I got back from the club. I was worried about Meech. If I wasn't where I was when that shit went down, he wouldn't be here. I shot at the same time Lil Man did, knocking the gun out of his hand. I thank God

Meech wore that vest. Our peace and quiet didn't last long. Ol' Lil Man done popped back up. I knew he had come for that baby. Sorry for him though, because he didn't have shit coming but a slow and painful death. This time felt different though. He had left the city with a big chip on his shoulder, and waited five long years before he came back. He had something up his sleeve. We were not dealing with the same Lil Man. But I was ready. I hoped everybody else was, too.

Outlaw

"Money Man, I know what the fuck I saw. The nigga hit him in the chest with a sawed-off. Lil Mama shot it out of his hand and scooped Meech up."

"FUCK! FUCK! FUCK! Where the fuck did they go?"

"I shot one of them niggas with dreads last night. I saw him in the club standing next to Haiti Redd. If he didn't have shit to do with it, oh well. Did you see that nigga Lil Man?"

"Yeah, I saw that pussy. I don't know what the hell he came back for. He must wanna die, so let's help him. I want you and Slim over here in the morning."

"A'ight."

I hung up with Money Man and called Slim.

"What's up, Outlaw?"

"You okay, nigga? I didn't see you when we got it cracking in the parking lot."

"I saw you though. You popped that dude with the dreads in the forehead. I hit one of them dread-heads with a bottle and got little. Did you see that nigga D Money?"

"D Money?"

"Yeah, he was with Haiti Redd."

"You mean that nigga Lil Man?"

"That's the nigga Lil Man y'all been talking about?"

"Yeah, that's him. We gotta make sure we send his ass back to Miami bloody."

"Okay then, that's the plan. I'ma get up with you in the morning."

"Meet me at Money Man's."

D Money

"Aw shit! That hurts, girl."

"Shut up and let me clean it for you D. Sit still, damn it."

That bitch Lil Mama shot me. This was not how I wanted my presence felt. The bullet went straight through my hand, but Goddamn it hurts. Now that they know I'm back, I need to hurry up and get my daughter before they hide her. My cousin, Khadijah, was back in her religious wear walking around with a scowl on her face.

"Why are you pacing the floors like that?"

She looked at me and rolled her eyes. I laughed at her stupid ass.

"I know why you're mad."

"Why am I mad, D?"

"You mad because you was talking shit, and that old-ass lady knocked yo' ass out."

"Fuck you, Derrick. I got something for that old bitch and everybody else who thinks I'm a punk."

She looked at me with a look that I didn't like.

"Bitch, don't look at me like that. I'm not gon' punch you. I'ma pop yo goofy ass."

After my hand was all bandaged up, I called Haiti Redd.

"Yo, cuzo, you good?"

"We can't stay long. They already know that me and you are connected. I'm going to go find my daughter. I suggest that you just pack up and close shop. We can make money back at home."

"I'm not going anywhere. I like Chicago. There's money up here, boy! You can take Khadijah and go on back. I got some help up here to shut down these lil' niggas for good. Have you hollered at Sal?"

"Yeah, I just re-upped last night before I went to the party. Who is his daughter?"

"I think she's supposed to be messing with the nigga you beefing with. Why?"

"Sal gon' be mad because I'm going to kill her if I catch Young slipping."

"Don't mess up what we got going on because you're obsessed with this nigga!"

"Fuck! What you talking about? You can stay up here if you want to. I'm out of here after I get my baby. In two days I'm going to make my move."

"A'ight, you do that. I'm about to go murk them niggas so I can have free reign over the city."

I could care less if his dumb ass stayed up here. If he didn't kill them niggas, they would surely kill him. I just wanted my baby. Nobody was going to stand in my way.

"Khadijah!"

"What?"

"Are you going to Jumu'ah today?"

"No."

"Yes, you are. I need you to stay close to JuJu and my baby."

She looked at her watch, grabbed her keys, and stormed out the door.

EIGHTEEN

Khadijah

Jumu'ah was the last thing on my mind. I wanted that bitch that hit me so bad. I got a good black eye, too. I called JuJu to see if I could get her to go to prayer services with me.

"Hey, girl! What you doing?"

"On my way to Tyshawn's school to talk to her teacher."

"Girl, what she do this time?"

"Her teacher said that she has a bracelet, and it looks really expensive."

"Really? I'll come along with you if you want some company?"

"Oh no, it's fine. Meet me at my house."

I got to her crib in no time. I wasn't worried about Jaw recognizing me. When I'm covered up, I look totally different. I had some makeup on covering my black eye. I grabbed my Glock .40 out of the glove compartment just in case.

JuJu

"Baby, get up. I gotta go get Tyshawn from school."

"For what?"

"Her teacher said she has a bracelet that looks really expensive."

"That lil' girl is something else. Poohman is lucky he like family, or else I'd send her lil' ass right home with him."

"I know, right?"

Knock! Knock!

Jaw got up and went to the bathroom, and I went to get the door. When I opened the door, I quickly noticed that Khadijah had a black eye. The makeup she had on did nothing.

"Oh, my goodness! What happened to your face?"

"What? Aw, this?" she pointed.

"Ain't nothing, girl. I slipped getting out of the shower."

I knew that was a lie because the bruise was on the inside of her face.

"You need to ice it."

I guess Jaw heard what we were talking about because he came out being nosey.

"Ice what?"

He walked into the living room and paused. I saw the weird look he gave Khadijah, but I didn't know what to say. He walked up on her like he was on a mission. He was definitely deep in thought.

"What happened to your face?"

I saw that the question coming from him made her uncomfortable. She put her hand up to cover her face.

"I fell in the shower."

I knew from the look on his face that he didn't believe her either. I didn't know what the hell was going on, but I was starting to feel uncomfortable myself. I felt like something was wrong. I just didn't know what.

"Come on, girl. Let's go see what this badass niece of mine has gotten into this time."

I kissed Jaw and headed for the door. He stopped me by grabbing my hand.

"What, babe?"

"I don't know, Ju. I think I saw her at the club last night with Lil Man and them niggas."

"Baby, are you sure? Wasn't you drinking?"

"Yeah, but!"

"Blame it on the Goose, baby."

"Man, Ju! I'm telling you that she looks like the bitch my momma hit last night."

I burst out with laughter.

"I gotta go!"

I kissed him and headed for the door. I wish I would have listened to my man.

Khadijah

I almost shit myself when Jaw looked at me the way he did. I thought I did a good job covering my eye, but I guess

I didn't. When he stopped her, I took that as my cue to head out the door. When I stepped into the hallway, I couldn't help myself. I had to eavesdrop. I needed to know what he was saying to her, so I listened.

"What, babe?"

"I don't know, Ju. I think I saw her at the club last night with Lil Man and them niggas."

Oh shit! He knows it's me. I grabbed my Glock out of my purse and clicked off the safety.

"Baby, are you sure? Wasn't you drinking?"

I paused for a second. If he got her to believe him, I was gonna have no choice but to kill 'em both right there. I hurried downstairs, walked outside, and got back into my car. I needed to make a call.

JuJu

Jaw's ass was tripping. I told him about all that damn drinking. When I made it to the car, I saw Khadijah hanging up the phone. I felt funny when I got in the car with her. The look she gave me really made me feel uneasy.

"Girl, I'm sorry about Jaw questioning you like that. He's still a lil' drunk from last night, I guess."

"Oh, it's cool. Liquor tends to cloud your judgment."

We rode the rest of the way to Tyshawn's school in silence. She must have had a lot on her mind. I know I did.

"Let me get on in here and see what the hell's going on."

I got out of the car and rushed into the building because it was starting to rain. When I reached Tyshawn's classroom, she was sitting by the teacher's desk. The teacher stood to greet me.

"Hello, Ja'ziya. How are you?"

"I'm fine. What's this meeting all about?"

I wasn't there for small talk.

"Well," she pointed and handed me a diamond bracelet that read *Daddy's Little Girl*.

It was blinged the fuck out. What the hell? This muthafucka was off the chain.

"Tyshawn, where did you get this from?"

She looked at me with those big ol' pretty hazel eyes and smiled.

"My daddy gave it to me."

"When?"

I just didn't believe that Poohman would buy her this bracelet. Actually, I could, because on her third birthday he bought her a pair of five-karat diamond earrings.

"When did he give you this?"

"When we was on the couch yesterday. I heard a knock at the door. You was asleep, so I went to see who it was. I opened the door, but nobody was there. There was a box on the ground in front of the door with a pink bow wrapped around it."

"I'm going to have to have a talk with him sooner than later."

What the hell was he thinking? This is Chicago. If a nigga will rob his own momma, what the hell you think would happen to a five-year-old little girl walking around with this bracelet?

"Okay, thank you, Ms. Jones. I'll take care of this."

Khadijah was still on the phone when I got back to the car. It must have been important, because when we got in the car she got out in the rain. My red flag was starting to rise on this bitch. What the fuck did she have to hide? I was starting to feel paranoid around her. I hoped it was the baby.

NINETEEN

Young Meech

For the last two nights I had been having nightmares. I knew that one day I would see Lil Man again. I just didn't think it would be at my damn party. I was glad I decided to wear my vest. That ugly muthafucka shot me in the chest. Thank God, that Lil Mama's ass is always in the wrong place at the right time. It was about to go down in the city. This time I didn't feel too confident. We were up against Lil Man and a whole bunch of niggas we didn't know. Money was surely about to slow down as the bloodshed rose.

Ring! Ring!

It was a private call.

"Who the fuck is this?"

I heard that familiar giggle.

"Young, my boy, I see you're still alive? Damn it. I wanna see you bleed to death. Can you help me make that happen?"

He started giggling again.

"Yeah, bitch, I'm always one step ahead of all you goofy-ass niggas. You're the one who's gon' die when I see you."

"You can't kill me, bitch. I'm God!"

I saw that this nigga was still a damn nut.

"Fuck you, nigga. I'ma see you in the streets. I promise I won't keep you waiting."

I was about to hang up on him, when he called out my name.

"Young?"

"What?"

"I'ma kill yo' bitch while you watch, and then I'ma blow your brains out."

I didn't even bother to respond. If the nigga was capable of getting my number, he was capable of finding my crib. But I got something for his ass this time.

"Hey, BeBe, come here."

"Yes, baby."

"I need you to stay out of the limelight for a while. Shit is about to go down, and I don't want you to get caught up in the middle of nothing."

I could tell that she didn't like what I had to say. I really didn't give a fuck either.

"Do you know who my father is? I'm not laying low from shit. Let's send them niggas back to where they came from in body bags."

"First off, yo' pops ain't even rocking with you right now. Do what the fuck I said. It's my job as your man to keep you safe, and that's what I'm going to do."

She rolled her eyes and walked off. Why the hell do women have to be so damn difficult?

D Money

I had been watching Young Meech's crib ever since I touched back down in the city. I called him just to fuck with his head some. I knew the nigga hated me with a passion. That was his downfall. He hated me so much that he let it cloud his judgment. You should never hate a person that much. Even after he murdered a few of my family members, I didn't hate him that much. I just returned the hate.

I was just about to pull off, when out came his bitch. Damn! She was definitely an upgrade from that dick-tease Tyesha. Shorty was fine as hell. I had to shake my head at Young's carelessness. He must not really love his girl. If he did, she wouldn't be out and about like shit is all good. I mean, really? You are at war with a very dangerous man and you let your bitch leave the house? It was time to send Young a message. It was time for me to do what I do best. Kill!

TWENTY

Jaw

"**P**oohman, bring yo black ass on. We need to go holla at Young Meech real quick."

"Nigga, I'm coming. You know my stomach's been tucked up since I got shot. I can't hold my shit, bruh. I gotta use the bathroom."

"Well hurry yo' lil' shitty booty ass up, lil' boy."

I called Young Meech to see if he was at home.

"Yo, what up, Jaw?"

"Me and Poohman 'bout to slide on you."

"Okay then. Money Man and Outlaw are on their way over here too."

About twenty minutes later I was coming down 67th Street trying to find a parking spot.

"Damn! I hate coming over here. Can't never find no damn parking spot."

Finally after circling the block for ten minutes, I was able to find a spot. As I was pulling into the spot, Poohman hit my arm.

"Ain't that Meech's girl right there?"

"Yeah, why?"

"Because I just saw that nigga Lil Man following close behind her."

"Man, you sure?"

"Hell yeah. Pull off. He's in the black Tahoe."

Shit! Why the fuck was she even outside anyway? I pulled right back out of the parking spot that took me ten minutes to find. As soon as I pulled off, somebody pulled in.

"Nigga, you better be right. It took me forever to find that damn spot. Call Meech."

"I already did. He's not answering."

I followed close behind the Tahoe wondering what he was thinking. This was bad.

"Poohman, we 'bout to have to kill this nigga."

"Good! It's about time, don't you think?"

Bianca

I don't know what type of girl Meech thinks I am. I'm not hiding because of no childhood beef he got with the next nigga. After he said what he said to me, I politely rolled my eyes, got my car keys, and got the hell on. When I get mad I hit the mall to relieve some stress. I popped in my Alicia Keys' "Girl on Fire" and hit the expressway. Today I was about to hit Michigan Avenue and tear a lining out of a few places. When I finally got downtown, there were people everywhere. Damn! I should have gotten a driver. Oh well. I found a parking garage and drove up to the top floor, popped my trunk, and grabbed my Prada sneakers. I was not about to shop 'til I dropped in no damn heels. As I was changing my shoes, I felt a cool breeze that caused the hairs on the back of my neck to stand up. I turned around and looked both ways. *Am I tripping? I could have sworn that I just heard somebody giggle.* I put my shit in the trunk and closed it. When I turned around, I ran smack dead into the boogie man himself.

D Money

I followed closely behind ol' girl. I was trying not to get too close. I didn't need to call for backup. I was going to do this tiny bitch wrong. I had to send a quick message to Young: Don't fuck with me. *Where the fuck are you going?* I followed this ho all the way downtown. She finally ended up turning into a parking garage. Better for me. I followed her all the way to the top floor. There weren't too many cars up there. I parked directly across from where she parked, and I took my time putting on my black gloves. I didn't want to leave any fingerprints. I watched her as she changed her shoes. She must have felt my presence because she turned around and looked back and forth. I couldn't hold back the giggle that escaped my lips. This bitch was completely unaware of the danger she was in. I walked up behind her as she was closing the trunk. When she turned around, she walked dead into the arms of the devil himself: me!

Jaw

"I'm telling you she went into that parking garage, Poohman."

"No she didn't, bruh. She went into that one."

There were two parking garages right next to each other. Shit!

"Okay, look! You go into that one and take the elevator to the top floor and walk down."

Poohman jumped out and ran for the elevator. I drove into the parking garage next door to him. I called Young Meech twenty fucking times, but he didn't answer his phone. Shit like this made me miss my Boost Chirp. I made it to the top level without hitting nobody's car. As I was turning the corner on my way back down, I saw Bianca and Lil Man going at it. I jumped out of the car and started running toward them. I didn't pay any attention to the gun in his hand.

Boom!

Bianca

"What the hell? Excuse you."

This nigga was all in my personal space.

"Do I know you?"

He gave me this creepy-ass smirk.

"You don't, but your man does."

"Okay, so what's that gotta do with me?"

I was trying to be tough, but at that very second I wished I would have listened to my man. I backed up somewhat, trying to put some distance in between us. As soon as I backed up, he took a few steps forward.

"It has everything to do with you."

I just knew that shit was about to go down, so I did what I would do if he was a female in my face trying to fight. I swung first.

Wham!

I caught that punk-ass nigga in the nose. Blood gushed out everywhere like a faucet.

"BITCH!"

Crack!

He hit me in my stomach almost knocking the wind out of me.

"UGGHH!"

I dropped to my knees and grabbed my stomach.

"Bitch, you bust my nose. Now I'm going to kill you."

He pulled out this big-ass gun. I was not about to die like this, especially down on my knees. I reached up and punched him so hard in his dick that my knuckles popped. As soon as I punched him, his gun went off.

Boom!

"Aw shit! My dick!"

I heard somebody yell and fall down. Who the fuck was that? I jumped to my feet and made a run for it. The dude that I hit was on the ground holding his nuts and moaning. I hit my alarm on my car and jumped in.

"Where the fuck you think you're going?"

He was on me like a fly on shit.

"Let me go!!"

I kicked and clawed, trying to get him off of me. He started clawing me back like a little-ass girl. I managed to grab my stun gun out of the armrest and placed it on his neck.

"B-b-bitch! I'm going to kill you!"

He fell back. I closed my door, started my car, and reversed.

Boop! Boop!

I ran over his legs as I zoomed out of the parking spot. I saw a dude lying on the ground when I was speeding past. He must have been the one to catch the bullet when the gun went off. Poor thing. I hit the gas and zoomed right on past him until I caught a glimpse of the guy's face. *Jaw? Oh my God!*

Poohman

The elevator ride was nerve-racking. My stomach was in knots. Man, I hoped I didn't have to shit. There was no bathroom anywhere near me. If I shit myself, Jaw was not gon' let me get back in his car.

Ding! Dong!

The door finally opened to the top floor. I quickly scanned around. There weren't that many cars around. I walked to the other end of the floor and looked around. Nothing! I was about to walk down to the next level, when I heard a gunshot.

Boom!

I ran to the side of the building that was facing the garage next door. I couldn't believe my eyes. Lil Man and BeBe were going at it like two UFC fighters, and from the looks of it, BeBe was whooping his ass. Ol' punk-ass nigga. I ran back to the elevator, but instead of getting on, I shot down the stairs two at a time. My heart was beating a million miles a second. *Who shot that gun? Where the fuck is Jaw?* I guess people outside heard the commotion because a little crowd had formed in front of the building that I was about to run into. I didn't miss a beat. I hit the stairs three at a time until I was on the top floor. I ran as fast as I could to where I saw them fighting. BeBe's car came flying around the corner almost hitting me. We both hit the brakes on our movement at the same time. It felt like the world started going in slow motion when I saw my boy lying on the ground facedown.

"Jaw, what the fuck, bruh? Get up!!"

I ran up to him and tried to turn him over. When I did, my heart broke into a thousand pieces. It was bad.

"FUCK! BEBE, HELP ME!"

TWENTY - ONE

D Money

I was in the hospital when I woke up. My whole body ached. I had a cast on my right leg, and my nuts felt like they were on fire. *How did I get here? Are the police waiting for me to wake up? I have to get the fuck out of here.* I saw my clothes and phone lying on the table. I grabbed my phone and made a call.

"Hey, cuzo, what's good? Haiti Redd, come get me."

"Where you at, bruh?"

I looked around for something that had the hospital's name on it. I found a piece of paper that read Northwestern University.

"I'm at Northwestern University. Come on, man. Hurry up."

"Nigga, I ain't from up here. Where the fuck's that at?"

"Google it, bitch. Just get here fast."

I hung up the phone and got ready to get the hell up out of there. When I tried to get out of the bed, I felt a pain that I had never felt before in my life. It shot up from the tip of my toes and went to my head. I couldn't do shit but scream.

"ARRGGGHH!"

The nurse came running into the room two seconds later.

"Are you okay, young man?"

"What the hell is going on? How did I get here?"

"You don't remember anything?"

"No! What do you know?"

"Some concerned citizens found you in a parking garage. You didn't have any identification on you, so we assumed you were robbed. Your leg is fractured in two places, and your other leg is bruised."

"I'm ready to go. Go get my discharge papers."

She looked like she was about to protest what I was saying. I went off.

"GO GET MY FUCKING PAPERS, BITCH!"

Her face turned beet red and she stormed off.

Young Meech

"Outlaw, I need you and School Boy Slim to go smash them Haitian niggas. Me and Money Man goin' go after Haiti Redd and Lil Man."

"We can handle that. The problem is that there are so many of them niggas up here now. We don't know where to begin. Haiti Redd and that other nigga have been laying low. I've been driving through his spots, and I ain't seen him or his car out there."

"A'ight! Then just shut the spots they got down permanently. You and Slim can take them niggas."

"What about his sister?"

"What about her? That bitch gon' die too!"

I got up from the couch and went into the bedroom to look for my phone. I thought I heard it beep. When I finally found it, I had almost twenty missed calls from Jaw. *What the hell is he calling me like that for?* I hit him back and got nothing. He didn't answer.

"Outlaw, hit up yo' brother."

I waited for a few seconds to see if he was going to pick up for him.

"I ain't got no answer."

I found Poohman's number and hit his line.

"Young, listen and don't say shit. Are Money Man and Outlaw with you?"

"Yeah."

"Don't say shit. Lil Man just shot Jaw. Get in your car and meet me at my baby momma's crib."

I was stuck.

"What you mean Lil Man shot him?"

"Man, just get here. I'ma tell you everything when you get here. Don't tell his brothers."

"Is it bad?"

"It's bad enough."

Poohman

I paced back and forth praying for my boy. He took one to the chest, and now it was lodged in his left shoulder. I didn't take him to the hospital because the nurses would have had to call the police and report the shooting. So instead I called my son's mother.

"What the hell you want, baby daddy. I'm on my way to work."

"Taya, I need you. Jaw got shot. I'm on my way to your crib right now."

"WHAT! No, take him to the hospital. I'll meet you there."

"No, Taya. I need you to fix him."

"Poohman, are you fucking crazy? I could lose my license."

"You won't get caught, man. I need you, man. Come on. No hospitals."

"I'ma kill you. Where is he shot at?"

"He got shot in the chest, but it's poking out of his shoulder."

"Okay, come to the house. You still got your key?"

"Yeah."

"I'm going to the job to get some supplies. Make sure you keep the pressure on his wound. I'll be right back. You owe me, nigga."

"Anything you want! Just save my friend."

It's not every day that a street nigga like myself has a baby momma that's a doctor. I met Taya my senior year in high school. She was a senior too. I got her pregnant shortly after we met. She was trying to abort my baby. I begged her not to. I told her that she could have whatever she wanted as long as she had my baby. She said she wanted to be a doctor. I hustled my ass off and paid her way through medical school. It took over $250,000 and seven years, but finally she got her degree. We broke up three years into her going to school, but I continued to pay her way through school. We are still the best of friends.

Back to the present, I was downstairs in her living room pacing back and forth waiting for her to come downstairs and tell me some good news.

Ring! Ring!

Shit! It was JuJu calling me. I couldn't tell her this shit right now. I took a deep breath and answered.

"What up, fat momma?"

"Hey, big head. Where is my man? He's not answering his phone."

I hated to lie to her, but in this case, it was very necessary.

"He's talking to a few of the workers right now. You good?"

"I'm okay, just bored. Ah, I knew I had something to talk to you about. The next time you buy your spoiled-ass baby a bracelet worth like $20,000, please let me know. You know niggas in the hood rob kids too."

"Who bought a $20,000 bracelet? I didn't buy her no damn bracelet, and if I did, it wouldn't have cost no twenty Gs. I don't even have jewelry worth that much."

"Are you sure? You know you stay high off that kush."

"Ju, I'm sure."

"Well, who the fuck gave her this bracelet that reads *Daddy's Little Girl*?"

"Daddy's little girl?"

"Yeah, Poohman."

"How Ah say she got it?"

"On the night of Young's party, she said I was on the couch asleep when she heard a knock at the door. When she got up to see who it was, there was no one there. The bracelet was wrapped up in a box in front of the door."

I held the phone for a few minutes trying to process what she was saying. My mind was all over the place until it clicked.

"Lil Man left that bracelet, Ju. Man, take Tyshawn and get the fuck up out of there right now."

"You're starting to scare me. What the fuck is going on?"

I was just about to answer her, when Taya called me.

"Ju, let me hit you back. Just do what the fuck I said."

I ran up the stairs as fast as I could.

"Taya, what's wrong?"

"I finally got the bullet out. He's lost a lot of blood, but he's going to be fine." I hugged her and held her tight. I was proud of her. She did what she said she was going to do, and she saved my friend. I sat down next to my boy and held his hand.

"He's going to be out for a lil' while. I'll make sure he's okay. You go do what you gotta do."

I left her house with one thing on my mind: murder! I picked up my phone and made a call.

"Gutta? Meet me at Taya's crib right now."

"What's good, my dude?"

"It's time to dust them thangs off and go to war."

"Say no more. I'm on my way."

TWENTY - TWO

JuJu

I don't know what's going on, but I do know that Jaw and Poohman's asses are up to something. I just know it. Poohman blew my mind telling me that he wasn't the one who bought that bracelet. Lil Man bought it? I didn't know what to believe.

Ring! Ring!

It was Khadijah.

"Hey, girl. What's up?"

"I'm bored out of my mind. You want some company?"

"I'm actually on my way out."

"Let me come chill with you until you head out?"

"You that bored, huh?"

"Girl, yes!"

"Okay, come on. Can you grab me a vanilla shake from Mickey D's?"

"I got you."

I went into the living room to check on Tyshawn. I stood there watching her copy the dances that the girls were doing on television. She was getting it too.

"Okay, baby, I see you."

She damn near jumped out of her skin.

"TeTe, you scared me."

"Whatcha doing?"

"Watching the dancing dolls juke."

"You got some moves on you, baby."

"I know I do. I'll murk Kayla and Camerin if I went up against him."

I fell out laughing.

"Come here, pooh pooh. Momma need to ask you a question."

She turned off the television and sat next to me.

"We have to leave for awhile. I think a very bad man is coming for us."

I kept it all the way 100 with her. Forget about lying to her. This shit was life or death.

"TeTe, is he my real daddy?"

Huh? Why the hell did she ask me that?

"Why would you ask me that, baby?"

She put her head down. She only did that when she felt like she was in trouble.

"Am I gonna get a whooping?"

I shook my head no.

"Khadijah told me that my real daddy wants to see me. She said that we are family and we'd all be together soon."

I felt like all the wind had been knocked out of me. Who was this bitch? I tried to remain calm, but I started shaking.

"Baby, why didn't you tell me she said that?"

"Because she told me not to. She said that you would get mad and whoop me. She gave me some money too."

I was floored.

"What else did she say?"

"She said my real daddy was a goon and he was coming back to shut shit down."

I wanted to fuck her up so bad. I didn't want her to know that I was on to her just yet. I called Young Meech. I wanted to see if she was the one Heidi punched at the club. He didn't answer. I tried again. Nothing! I called Outlaw.

"Hey, sis. What's good?"

"The bitch that your mother hit at the club, did she have dreads?"

"Um, I think so. As a matter of fact she did. Why?"

"I'll tell you later. I gotta go."

Fuck! Jaw was right. I wasn't safe. I told Tyshawn to go grab a few things, and I ran to my room and hit the stash spot. I was almost done when I heard the doorbell ring. Shit!

Khadijah

"You want me to do it now?"

"You said you've been talking to her, right?"

"Yes D, she knows who you are."

"All right. No more wasting time. Go get my baby. I got a few things that I need to take care of first. I'll be a few minutes behind you."

"You are all broke the fuck up. How?"

"DON'T FUCKING WORRY ABOUT IT! Just go get her."

Click!

I was so sick of his stupid ass. All he did was yell. Poor little girl. She was in for a rude awakening. Ol' bi-polar ass bitch. I called JuJu and made up a reason to visit. When she gave me the okay, I was up and out the door. I stopped at Mickey D's and grabbed her shake. I mean, hell, I could be nice. It was probably the last one she would ever have. I checked my .45 to make sure the safety was off. I rang the doorbell and waited. It took her a few minutes to come to the door. She finally answered the door after about three minutes.

"Hey, fat momma. Here is your shake."

"Thank you. Girl, you can't stay long. I'm in a hurry."

I didn't like her tone. I wondered if she knew who I was. Did the baby expose me? Impossible! I gave her little-ass lots of gifts and snacks and shit. I needed to get her in the crib. It looked like she wasn't going to budge though.

"Damn, fat momma, you okay?"

"I'm good."

"Well can I come in?"

She took a deep breath and stepped to the side. Pregnant-ass bitches are always so emotional.

"Where's Tyshawn at?"

I turned around to look at her.

Bam!

She hit me so hard in my nose that my eyes watered.

"What the fuck?"

TWENTY - THREE

Haiti Redd

After the clean-up boys came and cleaned my spot, I was back open for business. I underestimated that lil' nigga Outlaw. He made quite a mess. I had to send three of my partners' home in body bags. I won't make that mistake again. I don't give a fuck about the niggas he killed. He took my shit, and I want it back.

"Dre?"

"I want you and Mister to go with me to pay his mother a visit."

"You talking about the one that clocked yo' sister?"

I had to laugh at that one. Ol' girl laid out Khadijah's ass.

"You better not let her hear you say that. Bitch will fuck around and put a hex on yo' ass."

"You got the address?"

"Yeah. Grab some of them machetes over there. I'm going to make sure she tells me everything I wanna know. She's a disrespectful-ass bitch, so you know I want to make her scream a little."

I was about to make Chicago mine. This city is a gold mine. I was about to put these lame-ass Chicago niggas to shame.

Heidi

My sons had me on punishment ever since the club fight. I should be the one mad. I couldn't even get up with Rick Ross that night. I know he was peeping my style. I told them the club scene wasn't for me. I have another grandbaby on the way. It's time for me to chill the fuck out. I'm tired of punching muthafuckers. I kind of felt bad because Jaw said I started a war when I hit that girl. I don't see how. I think he made that shit up to make me feel bad. I'ma hold my own no matter what. I will not tolerate disrespect.

Ring! Ring!

It was Lil Mama calling me. Over the last few months we had grown extremely close.

"What yo' skinny ass want?"

"Well hello to you too, crazy. I'm about to come over. I gotta tell you what happened at the club after you left."

"What happened, girl?"

"I'm about to pull up."

I hung up and was about to pour me a drink when I heard a knock at the door. *Damn, that was quick, Lil Mama.* When I opened the door I wished at that moment that I would have listened to Money Man when he told me to put a camera on my porch.

"Back the fuck up, bitch. Scream and you die."

"Who the fuck is y'all?"

Whack!

I fell backward onto my hardwood floor.

"That's for hitting my sister."

His sister? Aw shit. This that nigga from the club. How the hell did he find my damn house?

"Do you know who my sons are, nigga?"

"Yeah, bitch, we know. Fuck them punk-ass niggas. You better hope Jaw makes it."

He spit at me then laughed. *Hope Jaw makes it? From what?* He and two more dudes stepped in my house and closed the door.

"Bitch-ass nigga, you better kill me now!"

He laughed like that was the funniest thing in the world.

"Oh, I intend to. Let me show you how us Haitian boys get down."

I started sweating when he pulled out this big-ass machete.

"I'ma cut you up, piece by piece."

I ain't never heard no sick-ass shit like that before. This boy was special. *Oh Lord, I have to get the fuck away from him. Help me please.*

Lil Mama

"Damn, Heidi, answer the damn phone."

I hung up and circled the block again. She gets on my fucking nerves. She knew I was coming. I finally found a parking spot like a half a block away. I was almost to the door when Young Meech called me.

"Hey, baby."

"Ma! Lil Man shot Jaw."

"What?"

"Poohman told me they followed him while he was following BeBe. Jaw was trying to help her, when Lil Man's gun went off."

This is the last thing we needed.

"Okay, I'm at Heidi's right now. Let me go—!"

"No! Don't tell. Just go and grab JuJu and put her up somewhere. We think Lil Man is about to make a move and try and get the baby."

"I'm getting back in my car right now."

I ran full speed back to my car. I needed to hurry up and get to my niece. I hoped wasn't too late.

TWENTY - FOUR

Money Man

"I don't know where the fuck Meech's ass went. I'm hungry. Wanna go to Mom Dukes's crib?"

"Hell yeah, let's go. I got the munchies too. School Boy, you coming?"

"Hell yeah. I love yo momma's cooking."

I looked at him and shook my head.

"You cooking, nigga."

"Aw yeah? A'ight, let's go then."

I wasn't feeling right the whole ride over to my mom's house.

"Outlaw, you got your key?"

"Nope. I forgot it. Hit the alley. I'ma go through the basement window."

"Call Momma's phone to see if she answers. If she catches you climbing through her window, she's gonna stomp yo' ears together."

I laughed at the possible sight of that.

"She's not picking up."

I pulled around in the alley and parked in the neighbors' back yard. The house was vacant anyway. As we all started walking up to the back of the house, I heard a loud-ass scream. Me, Outlaw, and Slim all froze in our tracks.

"Outlaw, who the fuck was that?"

Tears came out of his eyes.

"I think that's Momma."

We all took off running for the basement window.

"Outlaw, somebody's in there with her. Be as quiet as you can."

We all climbed in the window and spread out. I went straight for my choppa that was under the couch. Outlaw ran to the back room and came out with a Desert Eagle and a .357 Magnum.

"Here, Slim."

I put my finger up to my mouth signaling for them to be quiet. We jumped when we heard the scream again. It was definitely our momma. She was in trouble!

Heidi

"GET THE FUCK AWAY FROM ME!"

I was screaming at the top of my lungs. This punk bastard was cutting off my clothes piece by piece.

"Call your sons and tell them to come home."

"FUCK YOU!"

"Keep screaming, bitch! I'ma cut your fucking tongue out and slit your throat."

"This is my muthafucking house. You hit me and now you cut my off my clothes? Untie me so I can show you how a real bitch from the Chi gives it up."

"You got a lot of mouth for somebody that's about to die."

I was about to say something else smart until I saw one of the niggas he came with holding my favorite bottle of liquor. I lost it when he drank straight out of the bottle. I knew I was about to die, but I had to say something.

"Hey, you bubble-lip bastard, get a cup."

He looked surprised. He opened his mouth to say something, but never got a chance. His brains flew out through his mouth.

Outlaw

"Money Man. No matter what, none of them niggas is leaving alive."

"A'ight. Let's go, baby boy."

I was the first one up the stairs. I stood at the door and peeked out. I was trying to see who was in my mom's house.

"Call your sons and tell them to come home."

"FUCK YOU!"

I knew that voice. It was Haiti Redd. How the fuck did he find her crib? It was showtime. I was about to burst into the room guns blazing until I saw another nigga walking toward the living room with Mom Dukes's favorite bottle of liquor. I knew she was pissed now. I pulled the trigger and watched the back of his head explode.

Boc! Boc! Boc!

I let off three successful rounds, dropping his ho-ass where he stood. Unfortunately for Mom Dukes, brown liquor and blood flew everywhere.

"Ahhhh! My fucking white carpet."

"Money Man, grab Momma."

I saw Haiti Redd duck off into the corner by the front door.

"Don't run now, nigga."

Boc! Boc! Boc! Boc!

Out of the corner of my eye, I saw Slim untying my momma. A short nigga with dreads crept up behind him.

"SLIM, LOOK OUT!!"

Boc! Boc!

TWENTY - FIVE

JuJu

As soon as she turned around I went for broke.

Bam!

I hit her square in her nose. I was trying to close both of her eyes. Pregnant or not. I'm not no punk.

"What the fuck?"

Wham!

"What the fuck, my ass, bitch! You know what this is? You related to Lil Man? You tryin' to take my niece?"

Whack!

"Not today, bitch!"

Tyshawn came running into the living room screaming: "TETE, NO FIGHTING. You gon' hurt the baby."

I was in a zone, so I didn't even pay her lil' ass no attention. Khadijah was trying to get up, but I kept stomping her ass back to the ground.

Kick! Kick!

"Bitch! How dare you try to take my niece?"

My big ass was out of breath. I started breathing hard and shit. I stepped back and grabbed my stomach. I guess all the excitement startled my baby boy. He was kicking like crazy.

He was probably imitating his mommy's moves. That a boy. Tyshawn ran over to me and hugged me.

"TeTe, I'm scared. I want my daddy."

I was about to tell her it was okay, until I heard a gun cock.

Click! Clack!

"Oh, you want your daddy? Let me call him right now."

Lil Mama

Why the fuck don't nobody wanna answer their phones? I called Poohman's phone.

"Hello?"

"Poohman, is Jaw okay?"

"Aw shit, Lil Mama. How you know he got shot?"

"My son, Meech, told me. Never mind all that. Have you talked to JuJu? She's not answering the phone for me."

He was quiet for a second.

"I told her to pack a few things and get up out of there. Meet me over there. Wait! My other line is beeping."

I hung up and put the pedal to the metal. *JuJu, please be okay.* I said a silent prayer and pressed harder on the gas.

Khadijah

I underestimated this bitch. She was quick for a pregnant bitch. All I could do was ball up and wait for a chance to grab my gun. I got my chance when she stopped kicking me. She backed away and started hugging the baby.

"TeTe, I'm scared. I want my daddy."

Click! Clack!

"Oh, you want your daddy? Let me call him right now."

I had JuJu's undivided attention now. This lil' girl was a trip. For her to be only five years old, she was too grown up.

"I want my daddy, Poohman, not Lil Man."

"Poohman ain't your daddy."

"Leave me alone before my TeTe beats you up again."

What the hell was I doing arguing with a child for? The last comment did piss me off though.

"Shut up before I shoot your auntie in the stomach."

I called my cousin.

"Hey, Cousin."

"Come to JuJu's place. I got you baby and Ju over here."

"Don't move. I'm on my way."

I hung up and stared at JuJu. I was mad as hell because I let her fuck me up. She was lucky she was pregnant. Well, maybe not. D was gonna kill her anyway.

Ring! Ring!

It was D.

"Where you at?"

"I'm on my way up."

I smiled and looked at JuJu.

"Guess who's here?"

JuJu

I knew that if Lil Man came here to get Tyshawn, me and my unborn child were as good as dead. While Khadijah was on the phone, I pulled Tyshawn close.

"Baby, I need for you to listen to me. I need you to sneak out the back door and go get some help."

She had tears in her eyes. Oh God, that almost made me break down.

"TeTe, want me to go get uncle Jaw's gun from up under the bed?"

I was shocked.

"How you know about his gun under the bed?"

"I was under the bed hiding from you one day and I saw it."

These damn kids today!

"No, baby, I want you to take my phone and sneak out the back door. Remember the fire drills we do?"

She shook her head yes.

"Do exactly what we do when we play fire drill. If I try to run with you, she's going to shoot me in my back. If you let Lil Man take you, he's going to hurt me."

Her little pretty eyes were wide open with fear. I hated to see her like that, but she was going to have to do what I told her to do. Khadijah's phone rang. I knew it was Lil Man.

"Go now, baby. Say you gotta go pee pee. I love you."

"TeTe, I gotta go pee."

"Go ahead, baby. Don't forget to wash your hands."

Khadijah hung up the phone and smiled.

"Guess who's here?"

God, please let my death be quick.

TWENTY - SIX

Money Man

"**M**oney Man, grab Momma!"

I was still in the cut waiting for the other nigga to reappear. When I shot ol' boy with the liquor bottle, the other two niggas scattered like roaches. Slim went to untie my momma, and that's when I saw him. The short dude with the dreads crept up behind Slim with his gun pointed at his head. Outlaw peeped him too.

"SLIM, LOOK OUT!"

Boc! Boc!

I hit the dude twice in the face. My momma was borderline hysterical.

"Get the damn tape off of me."

Poor Slim. He was trying to take the tape off of her. The funny part about it was she was naked from the top up. She was going off.

"Hurry up and get this shit off of me lil' boy, and quit looking at my titties, before I beat yo' ass."

Slim didn't say a word. His face said it all. My boy was beet red. I looked around but didn't see Outlaw.

"Outlaw?"

Where the fuck did he go? Not even two seconds later he came through the front door.

"Bruh, where the hell you go?"

"I chased that nigga Haiti Redd. That bitch-ass nigga can run. I lost him."

My momma's crib was a mess. I called our boy Low. He got a cleaning business.

"Look at my muthafucking house. Who's gonna clean all this shit up?"

We kinda just stood there. We knew not to say shit unless she said our names. She was venting. When she turned around and looked at me, I knew it was time to talk. It was so hard to look at her because she was still topless.

"Um, I called my boy Low to come over here and clean up this mess."

I put my head down to keep from laughing. If I cracked a smile, she was going to fuck me up, even while she was topless.

"What the fuck are my neighbors gonna say about this? I know they heard all the commotion. You little bastards stay in some shit. I know for sure that Molly from next door ain't gonna invite me over for tea and cookies no more. I'm sick of all y'all's dumb shit. The first time I get a friend that calls me for my company and not to see my damn link card, y'all fuck it up. Get this shit cleaned up, and get the hell out before I beat y'all senseless."

I knew she was really pissed, but damn. She ain't never put us out before. I looked at Outlaw, and he had the same dumb-ass look on his face as Slim. They were trying not to laugh. They better not. She would fuck them up. I had to try and smooth this out a little bit.

"Ma, we're sorry about all this. It'll get it cleaned up, just relax. Can you just do me a favor?"

"What favor is that, boy?"

"Can you please go put on a bra and T-shirt?"

Before she could respond, Outlaw and Slim started cracking up. That's their asses!

"Oh, so you bastards think it's funny!"

Whack! Crack! Bam! Boom!

"Now get the fuck out!"

I was in tears when we walked out the door. Slim was the first one to speak.

"Damn! Yo' momma hits hard as hell. She ain't have to hit me in my stomach. I damn near shit on myself."

I was laughing so hard that I had to hold on to the gate to keep from falling out. Outlaw was quiet.

"You good, lil' bro?"

He burst out laughing too.

"Not only did I get punched and kicked, but she did it without a bra or shirt on."

We all fell out laughing. The way we were laughing, you would have never known that we just laid two niggas down in our momma's crib. Slim lit a blunt.

On some real shit, y'all momma got some nice-ass titties.

I looked at him and shook my head.

"You is a nasty-ass lil' boy!"

TWENTY - SEVEN

D Money

"**W**ell, hello, JuJu. I see you let that nigga get you pregnant. I wish that was my baby."

She turned her nose up at me like I was insulting her.

"I don't know what the fuck you're looking like that for. I look better than your black-ass nigga. You better hope that baby don't come out looking like his ugly ass. Anyway, I bet you thought you'd never see me again, huh? You thought I was gonna let you bitches get away with stealing my baby?"

"Ain't nobody steal shit. JoJo left her with us."

"Aw yeah, JoJo. She could suck a mean dick. Can you suck dick?"

"What? Fuck you, Lil Man."

"MY NAME IS D MONEY! Lil Man died a long time ago, and I would love to fuck you. You know what they say about pregnant pussy?"

I had to giggle at that one. I could see I was scaring her. She probably thought that I was going to rape her or something. Luckily for her I didn't want none of her raggedy-ass pussy. I just wanted my baby.

"Where's my baby, Khadijah? Where's she at?"

"She went to the bathroom right before you came in."

I picked up a picture that was on the table. It was a picture of JuJu, that crazy bitch ReRe, and my baby. She was so cute in the picture.

"JuJu, where the fuck is ReRe's crazy ass at?"

"She's on her way over here, so you better leave now. You know how she gets down."

"You better hope she doesn't come. If she does, she gonna discover your mutilated body."

I was tired of playing games. I turned to Khadijah.

"Go get her and take her to the car."

She came back three seconds later, childless.

"Well?"

She swallowed hard and stepped back.

"Sh-sh-she's not in there."

"Where the fuck is she?"

I snatched JuJu up by her hair and punched her in the face.

"Where the fuck is she, bitch?"

This crazy bitch punched me in my nuts.

"URRGGGGHHHH! What the hell? My nuts! She pushed me down and took off running. Thank goodness Khadijah's ass was there to chase her. I couldn't run. My leg was in a cast.

"Khadijah, go catch that slut."

Khadijah went to grab her by the arm, but JuJu turned around and cold-cocked her dead in her eye.

Wham!

I had seen enough.

Boc! Boc!

She froze.

"Get the fuck back over here before I shoot you in the stomach."

I guess those were the magic words because she came right back. Meanwhile, Khadijah was nursing her now swollen eye. I laughed at her.

"That's the second black eye you done got this month."

"Fuck you, D."

"Since it looks like my baby ain't here, I guess I'ma be taking you JuJu."

I picked up my phone and made a call.

Poohman

"Hold on. My other line beeping."

I clicked over from Lil Mama to answer JuJu's call.

"JuJu, why—?"

"Daddy, come get me."

It was Tyshawn. My baby was in tears.

"Baby, slow down and tell Daddy what's the matter."

"The lady, Khadijah, came over, and TeTe beat her up. She told me my daddy was coming to get me. I told her I wanted my daddy, Poohman. Then TeTe told me to take her phone and sneak out the back door. When the mean man was at the door, I said I had to pee."

My heart was beating so hard I could barely hear her talking.

"Baby, where you at so Daddy can come get you?"

"I ran down the back stairs, and now I'm at the store across the street from TeTe's apartment. Come get me, Daddy so we can go get my TeTe, please."

I had to choke back my tears.

"Daddy's on the way, baby. Just stay in the store."

"Okay, Daddy."

I hung up and floored it. *That son of a bitch. FUCK! If something happens to JuJu, my boy is going to flip the fuck out.* My baby got the hell out of dodge. I'm so proud of her. I just prayed that he didn't touch JuJu. My ringing phone interrupted my thoughts. I answered it thinking it was my baby again.

"Hello, baby. Daddy is—!"

"Daddy? That's MY baby!"

I pulled the phone away to look at the number. It was private, but I heard Lil Man loud and clear.

"Man! Dude, if you touch—!"

"What you gon' do pussy? Check this out, playboy. You got twenty-four hours to bring me my baby, or I'ma take this bitch back to Miami with me and drop her off in the

Everglades with some hungry-ass alligators. I'm sure they'll get full of this bitch and the bastard she's carrying."

I had to pull over. I knew this sick muthafucka would do some shit like that.

"Man, let that girl go. You wanna beef? Leave that shit between us men. You—!"

"Twenty-four hours."

Click!

FUCK! FUCK! FUCK! I pulled up to the candy store and jumped out to go grab my little girl. As soon as I walked into the store, she ran to me.

"Daddy, I thought you weren't coming."

I held her tight as I walked out of the store. When I had her buckled in, the questions started.

"Are you and Uncle Jaw gonna save my TeTe and her son?"

Son! I didn't even know she was having a boy.

"How you know it's a boy?"

"Duh, Daddy. That's my bestie. She tells me everything!"

I had to fix this shit. My boy would ride for me if I wasn't capable of doing it for myself.

"Daddy, is my TeTe gonna die?"

"No, baby. Don't say that. I'ma save her, okay?"

"Okay!"

God, I hoped I was right.

TWENTY - EIGHT

Bianca

I felt horrible that Jaw took a bullet for me. I should have listened to Young Meech when he told me not to leave. I checked my phone and saw that I had fifteen missed calls—all from my man. I was dreading this call, but I might as well go and get it over with.

"Hey, baby."

"BeBe, you good?"

His voice was full of concern. That was a good thing. Yes, honey, I'm good. I—!"

"You're fucking hardheaded. I told yo' dumb ass to stay in the house."

Damn! So much for sounding all concerned.

"Well, okay. I know you're mad, baby. I should have listened."

"I think you should go home with your family until this war is over. I can't protect you if you don't listen to me."

"I can't go home. My daddy don't want nothing to do with me, remember?"

"Tell him you're done with me."

I couldn't believe my ears.

"Are you serious?"

"As a heart attack. We are done!"

Click!

"Meech?"

He hung up on me. This muthafucka just broke up with me and then hung up the phone in my face. I had never felt more disrespected before in my life. I picked up the phone and made a call.

"Hola, BeBe."

"Manny, can you talk?"

"Si."

"I have an issue. I need your help."

"Anything for you, señorita. Meet me at our spot. Your father has been a very busy man. Your boyfriend is in danger. He uses the Haitian people to try and kill your boyfriend and his crew."

I was going to fix this. Meech was about to find out that I was his true ride or die!

Lil Mama

I was pulling up in front of JuJu's place when Poohman called me back.

"Hey, I'm here now. Let me call—"

"She's not there."

"You got her already?"

He got quiet. I didn't like the silence at all.

"Um, Lil Man took her."

"What? Wait a minute! He took her where?"

"Come to my crib right now."

"Fuck coming to your crib. I have been driving all over the city today. I'm tired. Tell me what the hell is going on, damn it."

I was livid. I looked in the mirror, and I was foaming at the mouth.

"He said I had twenty-four hours to give him his baby or else he was going to take JuJu back to Miami with him."

"MIAMI?"

I could tell it was more.

"And?"

"He said that he was going to drop her off in the Everglades and let the alligators get her."

Aww, not my baby. She's pregnant for Christ's sake. I lost it.

"THEN GIVE HIM HIS FUCKING BABY!"

I really didn't mean to say that, but, hell, I was definitely feeling it. I mean I love that little girl like she is my real niece, but damn it, JuJu is my real niece and my heart.

"What? No, Lil Mama. I'm not giving that nigga nothing. This is my baby. I'm raising her."

"We are raising her. Listen to what the fuck he said. He wants his baby, and if you don't give her back, we are going to lose two lives."

"I can't give her back, Lil Mama."

"So, what? It's fuck my niece and the life of her unborn baby?"

"Hell naw. We gon' get JuJu back alive and well."

"Don't gamble with my baby's life. If she dies, you will too!"

I was now in tears.

"I'm about to call ReRe because clearly you not hearing me."

I hung up on him and called ReRe. She didn't pick up. Damn it! I had to do something. I wish I could call Boo, but I'm not fucking with her petty ass so I called somebody who I knew would help.

"Hello?"

"Heidi, I need you."

I broke down.

"What the hell is wrong with you? I need you, too. You not gon' believe the day I had. What the hell happened to you coming over?"

I told her what was going on, and she snapped.

"Not my damn grandbaby and my daughter-in-law. Come get me right now!"

Twenty minutes later I walked into a war zone. Her living room was a mess.

"Girl, what the hell happened in here?"

146

When she told me about the Haiti Redd boy cutting off her clothes, I couldn't hold back the laugh that escaped my lips.

"Why the fuck does everybody think that shit is so funny? That little ugly, funky-breath bastard violated me."

"So how you get away?"

"My sons and Slim came through and put them niggas' dicks in the dirt. But Haiti Redd got away."

I braced myself for her reaction.

"We might have to go to Miami."

At first she was all happy and shit, until I hit her with the rest.

"Lil Man wants his baby back in twenty-four hours, and if he don't get her, he's going to take JuJu to Miami and feed her to the alligators in the Everglades."

"Miami ain't our city! We don't know shit about Miami."

"Fuck that! I'm going to get my baby wherever he takes her!"

"Just let Poohman and the rest of them do what they do best. We'll get her back before he tries to leave."

She was convinced, but I wasn't.

"Jaw is not going to let this shit happen."

She didn't even know that Jaw got shot. I hated to be the bearer of bad news, but she needed to know.

"You might wanna sit down. I got something to tell you."

"Sit down? What do you gotta say to me that requires me to have a seat? You know when people tell you to have a seat, it's bad."

"Jaw got shot!"

"OH LORD, TAKE ME NOW!"

This crazy bitch fainted. I was so sick of all this dramatic shit.

TWENTY - NINE

Poohman

I had to tell Jaw what was going on. He was doing better. He just couldn't walk for a long period of time. He knew something was wrong the second I walked in the door. I didn't have to say shit. My face said it all. I don't have a poker face.

"What, dude?"

How do you tell your friend—fuck that, your brother—that his pregnant girl is in the hands of the nigga that shot him?

"Lil Man got JuJu, bruh."

The pain in his eyes hurt me to the core. His chest heaved up and down, and tears cascaded down his face like somebody turned on the water faucet.

"Tyshawn got away and called me. Lil Man also called me and told me I got twenty-four hours to bring him his baby or he was going to take JuJu back to Miami and drop her off in the Everglades with the alligators."

I had to sit there and watch my best friend sob like a baby. I cried with him.

"Man, Poohman. I'm not nothing without that girl. She's having my baby. I took her virginity. THAT'S MY WIFE, BRUH!! I don't even know what she's having."

Damn! Shit was going to get worse before it got better. I had to tell him. I cleared my throat.

"I-I-It's a boy."

He just looked at me.

"A boy?"

I shook my head yes.

"How soon can we leave?"

It was my turn to stare. I just looked at him with the dumbest look on my face. Clearly he was in no condition to go to war. Not even a small one.

"You can't."

"Nigga, don't tell me what I can't do. Tell me what you gon' help me do."

"We ain't got no connections in Miami."

"Yes we do. Just worry about rounding up our niggas. Call Gutta and tell him it's his time to shine. I need him and his gunplay. I'm 'bout to make a few calls. Tell Taya to load me up on the pain medication."

I had a bad feeling about this mission. Jaw was not 100 percent, and we were about to tread in unfamiliar territory. They'd spot us a mile away. When he stood up, I could tell that he was hurting. I had his back though. If Miami was going to be our final resting place, then so be it. We weren't leaving without JuJu. He hung up his phone and looked at me.

"My people said they gon' meet us in Miami."

I got my thoughts together and called my troops. *Miami here we come. We shootin' niggas and taking names later.*

Young Meech

I had to have an emergency meeting with my crew. I needed to tell them about Jaw and now JuJu. Poohman told me that we might have to go to Miami and get JuJu. I was ready. When I finally got back to my crib, all eyes were on me. Outlaw was the first one to speak.

"Young, where the hell you been, boy? You not gon' believe the day we had."

I let him tell me without interrupting him. For the next half hour I was stuck.

I had to hold on to my stomach from laughing so hard at what he told me about Heidi.

"Who were them two niggas y'all murked?"

"I don't know. They wasn't at the club though."

"Damn! How many family members these ugly-ass niggas brought with them?"

"Shit, enough. I think I know where he's laying his head at though."

"Okay, we can make that move. I just got something else to tell y'all real quick."

When I said that, everybody stopped moving. Slim paused the game, Money Man hung up the phone, and Outlaw got off of the computer. All eyes were on me, their leader. I had to handle this like the boss I was.

"Okay, first off, Lil Man followed my girl and attacked her. She fought him back. Poohman and Jaw were on the way over here when they saw him following her. So they followed him instead of coming upstairs. Jaw was running to help her when Lil Man's gun went off."

Money Man put his head in his hands and put his head on the table. I continued.

"The bullet hit Jaw in the chest."

Outlaw didn't even bother to hold back his tears. I stared at him for a few seconds, trying to figure out what he was thinking. He stared me back in my eyes. I was definitely looking into the eyes of a cold-blooded killer.

"He's good though, but Lil Man got to JuJu and took her. If we don't give him Tyshawn in twenty-four hours, he's going to take JuJu back to Miami with him and feed her to the alligators."

Slim's ass actually threw up.

"Damn, nigga! You a'ight?"

"I'm good. So you saying we gotta go to Miami to get JuJu?"

"That's exactly what I'm saying. Slim, you went to school there. What are we up against?"

"A disaster. Haiti Redd got Miami in a headlock. If he makes it back to Miami with her, we ain't got a snowball's chance in hell."

"Okay then, we get him here. What about his sister?"

"Aw, man, that bitch. Just keep that ho away from me. Kill her too."

Slim was really scared of ol' girl. I started laughing.

"Slim, don't tell me you're scared of that bitch."

"Man, hell yeah. Any bitch that can put a spell on you and keep your dick from getting hard is a nightmare. That bitch is my boogie man."

"So let's make the move on Haiti Redd quick and easy. We need our strength for Miami if we gotta go there. They fucked with the right ones today."

This was the test that I needed. We needed. If we could go to the devil's playground and shut shit down, we were going to be unstoppable.

THIRTY

Haiti Redd

"**D**amn! She's cute. What's yo' name?"

She rolled her eyes at me and turned her head.

"Well, fuck you then, bitch!"

"Fuck you too. Ol' funky breath-ass nigga."

"I can't stand these stuck-up-ass Chicago bitches. D, what you gon' do with this ugly-ass ho?"

Before D could respond, shorty went off.

"UGLY? You must be talking about the bitch that had you, because ain't nothing over here, monkey."

I smiled at her ass because I liked that slick mouth she got. But D didn't like it, because he grabbed her face and applied pressure to both sides of her cheeks.

"Watch your mouth, Ju. I will not let you disrespect a boss-ass nigga like my cousin. You are in the presence of some real boss-ass niggas. You better show us some respect."

He put his hands down and was about to limp away, until she opened her mouth.

"Bosses? Where the fuck they at? You? Nigga, please. You think because you went away and grew up that you are the man now? You are still the same pissy-ass lil' boy whose mother is his grandmother."

Oh shit. This girl must really wanna die. I jumped up and got in between them just in time. D pulled his gun out and pointed it at her stomach.

"BITCH! I'll shoot you in the stomach right now. Say something else."

I didn't give a fuck what happened to her. I just didn't want him to shoot her in her stomach in front of me. I was gonna have to clean that shit up. I looked at her and gave her the silent shut-the-fuck-up look. I thought I would see some type of fear in her eyes. I didn't know this bitch was gangsta. Either she was really stupid or really crazy. Whatever she was, I wanted her to shut the fuck up.

"Don't say shit else. If you do, I'ma tape your mouth closed."

Under different circumstances, I'd have loved to wife this ho. D limped off, and she ice-grilled him the whole time. Oh yeah. She was definitely my type of girl. Crazy!

JuJu

A million things were going through my mind all at once. Did Tyshawn make it to the store? Did she call Poohman? I was scared out of my mind right now. Of course, I was not about to let these niggas see me sweat. Lil Man was staring at me so hard that it made me uncomfortable. Then there was this ugly, funky-mouth-ass nigga with red dreads. He looked a lot like Khadijah's backstabbing ass. I was so glad I beat her ass. I knew that I didn't have long to live. Lil Man kept saying that the alligators were going to love the taste of me. He said that they loved rotten meat, so since I was a rotten-ass bitch, they would surely swallow me whole. I was trying to mentally come to terms with the fact that my life was about to be over, when I looked up and saw the nigga they call Haiti Redd staring at me.

"Damn! She's cute. What's yo' name?"

I rolled my eyes at him and turned my head, trying to dodge his hot-ass breath. *He gon' get salty and start talking shit.*

"Well fuck you then, bitch!"

I couldn't hold my tongue any longer.

"Fuck you too. Ol' funky breath-ass nigga."

We went back and forth until Lil Man grabbed hold of my face and squeezed my cheeks together.

"Watch your mouth, Ju. I will not let you disrespect a boss-ass nigga like my cousin. You are in the presence of some real boss-ass niggas. You better show us some respect."

When I tell you I went in on his ass, he was so mad he pulled his gun out and pointed it at my stomach. Haiti Redd jumped in between us. I didn't expect that, especially since

I had just cursed his ass out. I was at a loss for words. I shut the fuck up because I didn't want him to shoot me. I bit my tongue so hard it bled in my mouth. When he walked away, I couldn't help myself. I mugged him so hard. He mugged me right back. Dirty-ass bitch! He stopped and turned around. My heart rate sped up because I thought he had changed his mind and was now about to shoot me. He saw the fear in my eyes. He laughed at me.

"Oh, and by the way, I shot your ho-ass boyfriend, Jaw."

Nothing could have prepared me for that.

"You're lying."

He knew he had me as he continued.

"I have no reason to lie, Ju. I hope you don't think he's going to come and rescue you. Bitch, you're stuck with me, and if Poohman don't bring me my baby, I might just cut yours out and keep it."

I couldn't hold back the vomit that had shot up to my throat from my stomach. I threw up all over the floor.

"Haiti Redd, clean that shit up."

I sat on the floor defeated. Was Jaw dead? He wasn't coming to get me? I had to get the fuck out of here and find my man. I looked up to see Haiti Redd staring at me. He had a look of sympathy in his eyes. If I could get him to feel sorry for me, I might have a chance. Lord knows that if I went to Miami, I was as good as dead!

THIRTY - ONE

Poohman

It was now or never. Outlaw told us about the hideout that he thought Haiti Red might be tucked away at. He also said that it was a possibility that Ju might be there. It was a long shot, but it was all we had to go on.

"Poohman, maybe she is there. If not, we can still eliminate Haiti Redd."

Lil Mama and Heidi were on the way over. I was still pissed at what Lil Mama said, even though I understood where she was coming from. I just couldn't give my baby to that maniac. For one, ReRe would put a bullet in my ass for sure. And two, I knew if I give her back, she would have a terrible life. That nigger wasn't capable of loving her the way I do. She is my baby—point blank period!

Ring! Ring!

It was Heidi.

"We're on our way up."

I hung up and looked at Young Meech.

"I just want you to know that yo' mom, Lil Mama, is mad at me. She told me to give Tyshawn back for JuJu."

He put his head down.

"I'm going to get JuJu back alive! I just can't give that monster my baby."

"I feel you. No need to talk about it. Let's just do what we need to do to get JuJu back."

Bianca

I was shocked when I called Manny's phone and my father answered.

"Hello, Bianca. Why do you still disobey me?"

"Daddy, what are you talking about?"

"I cut you off because you chose to put your life in danger. Then you turn around and use the loyalty that Manny has for you to have him steal my product."

Oh, my God! He found out. I didn't think he would. I felt so bad because I knew that him answering Manny's phone only meant one thing.

"Where is Manny?"

"You know the answer to that. In thirty years as my friend, he has never crossed me until now. I hope you can sleep at night knowing that his death is because of you."

My father was a cold man. The only person he was soft on was my mom. She wouldn't even speak to me because he said so. I didn't ask for this lifestyle. I just wanted to help my man claim his rightful spot on the throne. Was I so wrong for using Manny? I never thought that in a million years my father would kill Manny.

"You can make this right. Come home now and all will be forgiven. You are my baby, and I love you."

My daddy was not only coldhearted, but he was also a true psycho. I wished I would go home so he could cut me up into tiny pieces or some sick-ass mafia shit like that. I mean, I stole from him too. I was not safe in his presence.

"Daddy, I love him, and he loves me."

He chuckled that you-don't-know-shit-about-love laugh.

"He loves you, huh?"

"Yes, Daddy."

"Then why did you almost die by the hands of his enemy? A queen should always be protected by her king."

"Well why are you trying to help the enemies, Daddy? You put me in harm's way too."

"Aw, Manny told you, yes?"

"You are something else, Daddy."

"Have it your way. I will continue to supply the Haitians with my grade-A product. They will surely crush the competition. I will also make sure that they have an endless supply of ammunition so they can destroy your boyfriend and his little school-yard crew."

"What? I can't believe you are helping them."

"It's nothing personal. You will die with them. I will make sure of it. You are dead to me."

"You've been dead. You old-ass bastard."

Click!

I hung up and quickly put my plan in motion. I had some connections too. I was going to show Meech that I had his back.

Lil Mama

"Heidi, I'm not playing. Poohman better not say shit to me."

"Look! We're not on that. Let's just see what they have to say."

When we walked in the room, all eyes were on us. Outlaw, Money Man, and Slim put down their heads and started giggling. I didn't understand why, but Heidi caught on real quick. "What the fuck are you three stooges over there laughing at?"

Slim was the brave one to say something.

"Um, hi, Ms. Titties. I mean Ms. Walker."

"Ms. Titties? Little boy, you better forget you ever laid eyes on my titties. Pervert!"

Money Man hit the floor because he was laughing so hard. It took me a few seconds to remember the story she had told me earlier. When I did remember, I was about to laugh, until she cut me the death look.

"Don't make me fuck you up, Lil Mama."

"Oh, we can fight, as long as you keep your shirt on."

Everybody started cracking up.

"Y'all muthafuckas better get serious real quick before I punch every last one of y'all in the eye. Now who wants some?"

The laughing stopped. It was time to get serious, plus the mission that we were about to attempt required us to have 20/20 vision.

Outlaw

After we all got the goofiness out of our system, it was time to get down to business.

"Poohman, where is Jaw at?"

"My baby momma is making sure he's all right. He'll be here in a minute."

"Okay. I know where the nigga's at. In fact, nine out of ten times they are all there. I remember him saying something about a safe house. Since we're not giving Tyshawn up, we need a baby doll or something to throw him off."

Lil Mama went off.

"See, that's a dumb-ass plan. He's never gonna go for that again. If he senses some shit is up, he's going to shoot my muthafucking niece, damn it!"

"Then let's go in guns blazing."

The more I spoke, the more agitated she became.

"Let's just give her back! Look who we are dealing with. He's a cold-blooded killer.

"I'm a killer too, Lil Mama."

"Yeah, but you ain't got my pregnant niece, Outlaw, do you?"

I couldn't say shit back because she was right. I was about to say something else, when Jaw walked in the room. He looked tore the fuck up from the floor up. My mother rushed to him, but he held his hand up, stopping her.

"I'm good. I heard y'all all the way from outside."

He looked at Lil Mama, who looked like she was on the verge of a mental breakdown.

"That's my baby boy she's carrying."

He paused to keep from crying. I was about to cry right along with him. I ain't never seen my big brother like that before.

"We 'bout to tear this fucking city apart. We can't give Tyshawn back."

Lil Mama was about to object, until he snapped.

"WE ARE NOT GIVING HER BACK, LIL MAMA. END OF STORY!"

The whole room fell quiet. You could hear a rat piss on cotton.

"Outlaw, where them niggas at?"

"They out there in the Gardens on 130th."

"Yeah?"

"Yup."

"Alright, look. Poohman, Money Man, Outlaw, and Slim are going to the Gardens. My boy Gutta is outside in the car with four of our other soldiers. Lil Mama, you and Heidi follow us out there. Ain't no set plan really. We gon' have to wait and see what happens. Let's just go out there and get my girl back safely. I knew this was going to be a deadly mission, but we ain't scared of death. We welcome that shit. The Chi City Boys ain't scared of nothing!"

THIRTY - TWO

D Money

It was 9:45 p.m. I decided to call Poohman to see if we could speed up the process. I didn't want to really hurt JuJu, but if they didn't give me back my baby, I was going to murder her ass!

"Poohman, what's good, nigga?"

"You got some balls, lil' nigga."

"Big ones too. Where the fuck my shorty at?"

"She's asleep. Where you wanna meet so we can get this shit over with?"

This nigga better not be playing. I was tired of the games.

"Meet me on Doty Road right off of 130th. Don't try me, Poohman."

"What kinda car you gon' be in?"

"What kinda car *you* gon' be in? I'll call you when I see you."

"I'll be there in forty-five minutes."

I hung up the phone and woke up Khadijah's ass.

"Get up and go with me to get my baby."

"What we gon' do with that bitch?"

"We gon' take her with us. If things go wrong, we hitting the highway. If I don't get my baby back, they'll never see this bitch again. We can keep her baby."

She smiled at the thought of that.

"I'm about to go wake that bitch up. We can take all of our shit since Haiti Redd's staying up here. Let me go put our shit in the car and wake her ass up."

I went to wake up Haiti Redd.

"Hey! In an hour, me and Khadijah 'bout to take Ju and go meet up with Poohman. If he bullshits me, we're going back to Miami tonight."

"Leave King, Dooky, Fudge, and Rambo here. We're not ready to leave yet. There's still some money out here. I'll see you in a few weeks."

I was tired of Chicago. This place didn't love a nigga like me. *Fuck this city!*

JuJu

I laid there pretending to be sleep. I couldn't believe that I was about to go out like this. Haiti Redd had fallen asleep next to me on the couch. When Lil Man came to wake him up, I did my best not to even breathe hard. The plan was set. If Poohman didn't bring the baby, we were jumping straight on the highway. I couldn't let that happen. When Lil man walked off, I tried my luck.

"Can you please give me something to drink?"

He looked at me and smirked.

"Now why should my ugly ass do anything for you?"

I forced a tear to fall from my eyes thinking that would win him over. He took a deep breath and went into the kitchen. Seconds later he returned with a Tropicana orange juice. He handed it to me.

"Thank you."

I took four big gulps of the juice and then offered him some. Surprised by my offer, he said yes.

"I kinda feel bad for keeping you here. Women and children ain't my thing."

He sounded so sincere.

"You can let me go."

He quickly shook his head no.

"Girl, I'm not about to die because of you. I'm on top of my game right now. I got the best work, an endless supply of guns, and hella bread. This ain't my fight. I'm just the enforcer."

"What if I was your baby mama?"

"You ain't though."

"Don't let him—"

I cut my words short when that bitch Khadijah walked in the room.

"What y'all talking about?"

He turned to face the television and unpaused the video game.

"Mmmmm, let's go bitch." She went to grab me, and I snatched away from her.

"Don't touch me, ho! I can get up on my own."

"Then let's go."

When I looked at Haiti Redd, he was staring at me. My pleading eyes didn't even move him. Heartless muthafucker! I hawked and spit on the floor next to his feet.

"I hope you burn in hell, pussy."

I stepped out into the hot summer night scared and shivering. There wasn't a soul outside. I thought that was kind of odd. We were in one of the last standing projects in Chicago. There were always niggas everywhere. Khadijah snatched my arm and led me to a black Tahoe.

"Get in."

I was glad I did, because as soon as I got all the way in, her fucking head exploded!

Lil Mama

We were parked in the cut. I could see the first few blocks from this angle. My stomach was in knots. I hoped they got her out safely if she was in there. Heidi was on the side of me, popping the shit out of her gum. I looked at her.

"What?"

"My nerves are shot. Quit popping that damn gum."

She rolled her eyes and turned back to look out the front window. Two seconds later she shrieked.

"What now?" she pointed.

"There go JuJu with that lady."

"WHERE?"

"Shhhhh. You're too loud. Right there."

I looked to my right, and sure enough, there was my niece. I was about to get out and run to her, until Heidi grabbed my arm.

"No, Lil Mama. Let them get her. If we see her, then you know they do too."

So we sat and watched. The bitch was rough with my baby. JuJu climbed in the truck. As soon as she lifted her last foot off of the ground, ol' girl's brains flew everywhere."

"OH SHIT!"

Young Meech

Outlaw was right about the hideout. We were all in position. Haiti Redd's car was outside of a building on block one. Poohman was waiting at the top of the bridge on Doty Road with an AR-15 rifle. Jaw and Outlaw were on the next block in the cut. Money Man and Slim were both 20 feet away from me. Gutta was on the roof across the street on the roof of a building with his AK-47. He had a mean-ass shot.

He was a Marine reject that wouldn't stop smoking weed, so they kicked him out of the Marines. He never lost his touch though. We weren't even there for 10 minutes when I saw Lil Man limp out of the house. I stared at him without blinking. He looked exactly the same but taller. I hated his fucking guts. I wanted to rush him and shoot him in the face at point blank range, but this wasn't about me. About two seconds after he came out, Khadijah came walking out with JuJu. My heart was beating so hard that I thought it was going to pop out of my chest. I gave Gutta the signal to take the shot. As soon as Ju got all the way in the truck, he popped off.

Pow!

Her brains flew everywhere. Me and Money Man rushed the building from the west, while Slim, Jaw, and Outlaw were two steps behind us. One dude came out of the shadows and let off a few shots. He had a big-ass gun but a terrible aim. Outlaw blew his legs off with a sawed-off shotgun.

"ARRRGGHHH, MY LEGS!"

He was screaming loud as hell until Jaw walked up on him.

Boc!

Jaw shot him in the head at point-blank range.

Damn was all I could say! He had this murderous look in his eyes.

170

"Outlaw, hit the door. That nigga, Haiti Redd, gotta be in there. Jaw, Ju's in that truck."

Jaw went for the truck, while me, Outlaw, Money Man, and Slim stormed the crib. Outlaw shot the lock off the door as we rushed the crib like the ATF boys.

"Kill everything moving!"

Haiti Redd

The look she gave me made me feel like shit, but so what. I'll get over it. I unpaused the game and lit my blunt. This special apps game was the real deal. I should have taken my black ass to the Army. I turned the sound up to drown out King's snoring. I was good into the game until I heard the back door fly open.

Boom!

Four dudes wearing all black rushed the crib. I thought it was the police until I heard one of them say, "Kill everything moving!"

I jumped on the floor and grabbed my .45 from under the table. King jumped up and hit the floor, too.

"Haiti Redd, what the fuck!"

I heard Outlaw scream, "There's that nigga, Haiti Redd. Go!"

Oh, they were coming for me? Okay, then let's get it.

THIRTY - THREE

D Money

Me and my homie, Flex, were in the Tahoe chopping it up, while smoking some weed laced with coke when all hell broke loose. I was feeling all tingly and shit. I couldn't quit giggling.

"Yo, ass-retard D. Pass that shit."

I passed him the blunt the same time I saw Khadijah and JuJu walking toward the truck.

"Flex, you gon' ride with me while I make the exchange?"

He pulled deep on the blunt.

"So, you not gon kill that bitch?"

I seriously thought about it, but I changed my mind.

"Not this time. I came up here to get my baby. I'll let Haiti Redd handle my lightweight."

The back door opened and JuJu climbed in. I was about to say something slick, when all of a sudden, my cousin's brains flew everywhere.

"What the fuck?"

JuJu tried to jump out of the truck, but Flex grabbed her by the hair.

"Pull off, D."

I started the car and went in reversed. I saw Jaw running toward the car with his gun pointed at the driver's side window. I smiled and drove off. I saw my boy, Dooky, lying on the ground dead.

"Damn, Dooky."

I couldn't believe my eyes. I had to get to the expressway. I zoomed down 130th street. I was almost there until a blue van cut me off.

"Who the fuck is that?"

Lil Mama

I watched in pure horror as Outlaw blew that boy's legs off. Jaw followed up with a bullet to the head. Damn! Them boys wasn't playing. The truck Ju got in reversed and busted a U-turn.

"Lil Mama, don't let them get away."

I was on it. I fired up my engine and stomped on the gas. I had to jump the curb to get in front of the truck. The Tahoe hit the breaks to avoid hitting me. I jumped out of the van with my pistol in hand.

"LET HER OUT NOW!!"

He turned on his high beams and blinded me. I then ran to the driver's side of the truck and opened fire.

D Money

Lil Mama jumped out of the blue van and ran up to my truck.

"AUNTIE!" JuJu screamed for her.

"Flex, get back there and shut her the fuck up."

I hit my high beams and tried to blind her ass. She came to the driver's side and started dumping.

Boc! Boc! Boc! Boc! Boc!

"Man, D, pull off."

I sat there smiling at Lil Mama. My entire truck was bulletproof. JuJu was in the backseat fucking Flex up.

"Quit girl!"

Whack!

"I don't want to hit you!"

Whack!

"Bitch, stop hitting me!"

I was tired of this shit. I turned around and hit her in the face with my gun, knocking her out cold. I threw my car in reverse and hit the gas.

Outlaw

"Slim, that nigga's under the couch. Shoot him."

Slim turned toward the couch and let his gun loose.

Boc! Boc! Boc! Boc!

I ran down the hallway to see if anybody else was in the house. It was clear. We didn't need a bunch of crazy, ugly muthafucking Haitians rushing us with all kinds of weapons and shit. I turned to leave, and a bullet whizzed past my head. It slammed into the wall.

"What the fuck?"

Click! Clack!

It came from the closet. I shot into the closet door.

Boom! Boom!

I walked up on the closet to see who I had shot. It was a nigga I didn't recognize. Damn! How many of these dread-heads are here? It was a war zone in the living room. When I ran back up front, I saw my boys shooting it out with some more niggas who I never saw. Haiti Redd managed to jump out of the front window.

"He's getting away!"

I was pissed. This dirty-ass nigga always got away. Not today though.

"Come on, y'all. Blow out of here. Haiti Redd's getting away."

Slim dropped the nigga he was shooting at, while Money Man and Young were already out the door.

Poohman

When I saw Gutta shoot that dread-head bitch, my adrenaline started pumping. I couldn't make my move yet. I knew my niggas were gonna handle business. I saw Jaw run after the truck trying to get to JuJu. It pained me to watch him do that. Lil Man reversed and tried to pull off, but Lil Mama's crazy ass blocked him in as she jumped out of the van and started dumping at his truck. Dirty muthafucker. The truck was bulletproof, but Lil Mama still emptied the clip at his truck. Man, that bitch is a beast. When Lil Man backed away and went the other way, I started up my engine. He had to pass me to get to the expressway. I wasn't gonna let him get away with JuJu. He flew right past me. I didn't hesitate to gun it right behind him. If he got away, we would never see JuJu alive again. I couldn't let her down.

JuJu

When I saw the blue van jump in front of us, I thought it was the police. I was ready to jump up and down for joy. But to my surprise, it was my auntie, Lil Mama. She jumped out of the van ready for war. I couldn't hold back my scream.

"AUNTIE!"

Lil Man got really mad about that.

"Flex, get back there and shut her the fuck up."

"Yeah, okay!"

He climbed back there with me, and I gave his ass the business. I went crazy on his ass. Shit! I was fighting for my life.

Whack!

I popped him square in the side of the head. We both paused mid-brawl when my auntie opened up fire on the driver's side of the truck.

Boc! Boc! Boc! Boc! Boc!

His friend was spooked.

"Man, D, pull off."

Lil Man had a crazy-ass looking grin on his face. I started punching Flex's ass again.

Whack!

"Quit, girl!"

Whack!

"I don't want to hit you!"

Whack!

"Bitch, stop, shit!"

The last thing I remembered before blacking out was Lil Man hitting me in the face with his gun.

(Lil Mama)

"DAMN IT! NOOOO!"

I dropped to my knees. He got away with my baby. I was on the ground and sobbing like a baby when Heidi came running up to me. At this point I was inconsolable.

"Come on, Lil Mama, you gotta get up."

I didn't budge.

"Girl, get yo' ass up before I punch you in the back of yo' damn head."

"Heidi, he got my baby."

"Poohman chased him. Now come on. We gotta get the fuck from 'round here before the police come and take our asses to jail."

She was right. I pulled myself up off of the ground. As soon as I was all the way up, I saw this nigga with red dreads coming our way.

"HEIDI, WATCH OUT! HE'S GOT A KNIFE."

He came out of the shadows carrying a big-ass machete. Heidi snapped.

"That's that muthafucker who cut off my clothes. You're a fucking pussy-ass nigga to do some shit like that."

"Which one of y'all bitches killed my sister?"

I didn't say shit. I didn't wanna make any sudden moves. Where the fuck was Money Man and the rest of them boys? I didn't have no more bullets in my gun.

"Where the—?"

My words got caught in my throat when a bullet flew through his left eye. Heidi screamed.

"AW, BITCH! LET'S GO RIGHT NOW!"

We jumped in my van and pulled off.

Young Meech

We lost Haiti Redd. We didn't get JuJu. That was the whole plan. We popped a few niggas, but that wasn't gonna bring JuJu back. We failed! We ran back to our cars and got the hell out of dodge when we heard the sirens coming. Everybody in the truck was silent. Nobody wanted to speak, especially while Jaw still had his gun in his hand. We knew we had fucked up. Jaw was the first one to break the silence.

"Where the fuck did Poohman go?"

"I don't know. Call Mama and ask her what happened."

He did and put her on speaker phone.

"Hello, Ma?"

"We 'bout to hit the expressway. Where y'all at?"

"What the fuck happened? Where is Poohman?"

"Well, I blocked him in and shot up the truck. He didn't get hit because the truck was bulletproof. He reversed and sped away, and that's when Poohman chased him."

I was on the verge of a nervous breakdown. I tried to relax knowing that Poohman was going to do everything in his power to stop them.

"That crazy-ass dude with red dreads ran up on me and Heidi in front of the building."

"What happened?"

"He was coming at us, until a bullet flew through his damn eye. We don't know who shot him, but we was thankful. Shit! He had a big-ass knife."

"Alright, Ma, we'll get up with y'all in a minute."

I was about to hang up the phone, when I heard them scream.

"OH GOD! NOOOO!"

We all jumped up in our seats.

"Ma, what the hell? Where y'all at?"

"We're by Gary Indiana on Interstate 65 south. Get over here right now. Poohman's car is wrecked on the side of the road."

I hit the gas, and we were on the scene within ten minutes. There were police and EMTs everywhere. I pulled over to the shoulder and jumped out to see where Poohman was. When I made it over to where the ambulance was, I saw them patching Poohman's head.

"Excuse me, sir, you can't—"

"Let me go. That's my brother."

I ran right up to the ambulance truck.

"Poohman! This is Meech. Boy, you a'ight?"

He was awake but in a daze. He looked at me and tears fell from his eyes.

"He got away, bro. Tell Jaw I'm so sorry."

The EMT man came over to me.

"All right, we need to get this man to the hospital."

The walk back to the car was the longest walk I had ever taken. When I got back in the car, I couldn't even look at Jaw. He was staring straight ahead.

"Is my boy a'ight?"

"He's good. He told me to tell you he's sorry."

Gutta called Jaw's phone, and Jaw put him on speaker.

"What up, bruh? You cool?"

"I'm good over here. I had to clean up a few more niggas before I got out of there. I'm on my way home. What happened? Did you get ya girl?"

"Man, you might as well pack a bag, nigga."

"We laying low?"

"Something like that."

"Where we going?"

"Miami."

"Aw, I forgot to tell you I took care of the dude with the red dreads. One less nigga we gotta worry about in Miami."

"Good!"

THIRTY - FOUR

Lil Mama

After we went to the hospital to make sure Poohman was okay, everybody came back to my crib. Jaw, Money Man, Outlaw, and Slim were all lying on the floor. Heidi and I sat on the couch while Young Meech paced the floors. I couldn't hold in my tears any longer. I cried. The thought of me not seeing my baby again was too much to bear. Poohman walked in the door looking fucked up. He didn't say a word, until Jaw finally spoke.

"Killing them niggas didn't mean shit because we didn't get my girl. Ain't no need to sit here and pout. Y'all already know what we 'bout to do, so get ready. If you don't want to go, say something now."

Nobody said a word.

"I called a friend that's going to meet us in Miami. Y'all got two hours to pack. Hurry up!"

JuJu

When I woke up, my hands were taped together. Flex was driving now, and Lil Man was knocked out in the passenger seat. I wasn't about to accept this shit. I looked around for something I could use as a weapon. I was about to give up, until I saw something silver by my foot. I used my foot to move it. Oh God! It was a phone. I looked at Flex to see if he was paying me any attention. He wasn't. I turned my body and lay on the seat like I was trying to get comfortable. Flex glanced at me but only for a second. When he turned back around, I grabbed the phone and texted Jaw. Lord, please let his phone be on.

Jaw

I went back to my crib and showered. My body was hurting, but not as bad as my heart. I couldn't think straight. The thought of not having JuJu in my life made me sick. I felt like I was suffocating. Damn, she was having my baby! I didn't think I had any more tears left, but when I thought about him hurting her I broke down. The hatred that I had in my heart for Lil Man was going to be the death of him. There wasn't a soul in the world that could stop me. *I'm going to murder that boy.*

Ring! Ring!

Thinking it was the guys or somebody else I ignored it.

Ring! Ring!

"What the fuck?"

I snatched up my phone and almost fainted. It was a text from a number I didn't know: "Baby, we are on the highway going to Miami. We 'bout to hit Highway 75 right now. Please get here. I love you. I hope you are okay."

Buzz! Buzz!

She sent another one: "He said he's gonna cut my baby out and then kill me. Don't let him do that. Please get to me. I love you."

I didn't wanna text back because I didn't want them to know she had a phone. I threw my shit on and quickly flew out the door. As soon as I opened my door, I ran smack dead into Poohman. He still had that big-ass bandage on his head.

"Boy, you need to be back in the hospital."

"I'm good, nigga. Let's go get my sister, man. I'm sorr—!"

"Don't trip, man, we gon' get him. What the hell happened?"

"After Lil Mama shot his truck up, he reversed and sped toward the expressway. I was on his ass, bro, I'm telling you. I rammed the back of his truck a few times. When I pulled alongside him, I tried to shoot out his tires. But the bastard clipped my bumper and sent me flying into the divider."

"Damn! I knew that was a hard-ass hit. Your car was totaled."

"I had on my seatbelt though."

We both started laughing, trying to ease some of the tension.

"You mad at me?"

"Naw, I'm mad at myself."

I showed him the texts that she had just sent me.

"You think he gon' kill her?"

"Not if we get to him first."

"Let's go then."

I headed out of the crib that I shared with my girl. I could still smell her perfume in the air. This was probably the last time I would step foot in there. If I didn't get her back, I wasn't coming back. If he killed her I wouldn't stop until I had that nigga's heart in my hands—literally!

Bianca

I called Meech's phone for the tenth time. Finally he picked up.

"What the fuck did I tell you?"

I was taken aback by his rudeness.

"I need to talk to you."

"I'm busy, BeBe. We done, man. Ain't shit to talk about."

"Look! My daddy killed Manny, and he's supplying the Haitians with drugs and guns."

"Say what?"

"You heard me. He found out I was getting work from Manny, so he killed him."

"Damn, ma, I'm sorry."

"He knows about Lil Man trying to kill me."

"How?"

"Because he's helping them."

"Look! When I come back from Miami, I'ma holla at you. There's too much shit going on."

"Why are you going to Miami?"

"Lil Man took JuJu."

"Oh no! Look! We got a crib in the heart of Miami. I got a lot of friends down there with connections. I'ma fly there and meet y'all."

I was hoping he didn't say no.

"It's gonna take us like sixteen hours to get there. What's the address?"

Yes! I gave him the address and booked my plane ticket.

"Meech, I love you, and I got your back."

"I love you too."

Young Meech

When we all made it back to Lil Mama's crib, I told them what BeBe said. Money Man couldn't stand her.

"Man, I don't trust yo' girl, bruh."

I let him have it. He had the right to voice his opinion.

"All right, look! We gon' take two trucks. Outlaw, Slim, Money Man, and me are gon' ride together. Jaw, Poohman, Lil Mama, and Heidi gon' ride in the other truck. We can grab Gutta on the way to the expressway. Jaw, didn't you say you had a friend in Miami?"

"Yeah. She's gonna meet us there."

We were about to head out, when my phone rang.

"Hello?"

"Young, my boy, tell Jaw that I'm going to keep his child. I changed my mind. I'm not going to kill it."

He started laughing. Jaw's face was tight as shit.

"Nigga, there ain't a rock that you gon' be able to hide under. We will find you."

"Oh, I'm not hiding. Since you pussies didn't wanna give me my baby, y'all can keep that little bitch. I want a brand-new baby."

"We'll see about that one."

He laughed again.

"Indeed we will."

Click!

"Let's go, y'all. I want y'all to know no matter what, we stick together. This ain't our city, so let's get in and out."

Heidi looked mad as hell.

"What's on your mind, Heidi?"

"Don't get me down here and get me killed, Goddamn it! I got shit to do and a life to live."

"All right, let—"

Knock! Knock!

I looked at Lil Mama.

"Are you expecting company?"

She didn't respond. When she opened the door, I almost shit on myself. I'm sure everybody in the room felt the same way. Heidi was the first to speak.

"Aw, hell yeah. ReRe's in the fucking building!"

ReRe walked in looking like the true killer she was. She mugged every last one of us. I felt very uncomfortable.

"Y'all let that bitch-ass nigga take my bestie, and nobody wanted to call me?"

Poohman walked over to her, and she gave him the look of death.

"What the fuck are y'all standing there for? Let's go get my muthafucking bestie!"

Chi City Boys Road to Destruction Coming Soon!

BOOKS BY GOOD2GO AUTHORS

GOOD 2 GO FILMS PRESENTS

**THE HAND I WAS DEALT- FREE WEB SERIES
NOW AVAILABLE ON YOUTUBE!
YOUTUBE.COM/SILKWHITE212**

SEASON TWO NOW AVAILABLE